Susan Moore

A STORY FOR THE TABLOIDS

2023

Susan Moore, A Story For The Tabloids

© Susan Moore, 2023
© Ir A Artemente, 2023

PUBLISHER
Artistic Agency
IR A ARTEMENTE
02-454 Warsaw
26 Szczęsna St.
www.iraartemente.com

ISBN 978-83-965986-5-3

PROLOG

One year ago

Amy Davis was waiting in the lobby of the large publishing house Empire Books, which was located in the heart of downtown Chicago.
Until now, she still couldn't believe the luck that had smiled upon her. She was only twenty-six years old. She didn't know what she should expect from this meeting, so she decided not to dress formally. She wore a black skirt before her knees and an ecru-colored blouse, which was made of shiny material. She tied her long dark hair into a loose bun. She always dreamed of becoming a writer someday, so she started writing stories from an early age. When she sent her text to a publishing house, she wasn't quite sure if they would want to cooperate with her. The message came enthusiastically.
-We want to publish your books. - She read a few days ago in a letter from Empire Books. - If you decide to go ahead, please make an appointment with Literary Agent Ralph Jones, who will give you more details. Amy was filled with happiness. Later that day she called the phone number for the publishing house indicated in the letter. In the receiver, she heard a friendly female voice. - This is Sarah Wilson how can I help you? - The woman asked over the phone.
-Good morning my name is Amy Davis. - She began uncertainly. - Ah good morning Mrs. Davis, we have been waiting for your call. - Said the woman encouragingly. - Really? - Asked a slightly shocked Amy. - I wanted to make an appointment with

Literary Agent. - Threw Amy suddenly when the woman in the earpiece unexpectedly interrupted her.

-Mr. Jones can receive you tomorrow around ten o'clock. Does this date suit you? - Yes, of course. - I will immediately send you an e-mail and give you all the details. - The secretary said at the end of the call and then cut the connection.

Now Amy was waiting outside the office where she was to meet her future Literary Agent. The comfortable leather armchair in which she was seated and the third tea offered by the secretaries made Amy begin to doubt whether fate could really smile on her like this. Her musings were suddenly interrupted when the office door opened. From there came out the woman, Sarah, who had entered there fifteen minutes ago to announce her. Amy wondered why they were making her wait so long. The gentle smile on the secretary's face made her breathe a sigh of relief. - Mr. Jones is waiting for you. - Said the secretary encouragingly. Amy slowly stood up and entered the office with a little trepidation. Upon entering, her gaze was immediately fixed on the man who rose from his chair at the sight of her. He was thirty-three years old. He was handsome in a navy blue suit and a light blue shirt could please any woman.

Amy didn't know how long she had been standing so still. Ralph Jones smiled and held out his hand to her to indicate for her to sit in the chair across from him. Amy woke up and slowly walked toward the man and sat down in the chair. She breathed a sigh of relief.

-Ms. Davis - Ralph began - Do I write you for a long time? - Ask in a poised tone.

-Mhm... A few years. I started writing stories when I was still in school. - Amy admitted with calmness.

- I've been working as an agent for a few years now and I know it well. My publisher and I have decided that your story is worthy of being published in our publishing house. I am confident that the book will sell well. - He communicated.
- What do you think? - Asked leaning slightly toward her with a seductive smile.
- I would like that very much. - Responded Amy, not knowing if she was doing the right thing by revealing her feelings.

- Good. - Said Ralph, mirroring his entire office with his eyes. Suddenly he clapped his hands. - In that case, why don't we have a cup of coffee and discuss the details? - Ask. - Great.- Said Amy trying to control the surge of joy that accompanied her.
Ralph averted his eyes and was already reaching for the phone receiver when suddenly his attention was focused on something completely different. He looked at Amy's slender legs for a moment.
He knew his immobility had gone on too long, but he didn't know how he was supposed to stop himself.
- What the hell is going on? He had never reacted this way to any of his clients before. - He thought and then managed to come back to reality. He grunted.
- Maybe we can go for coffee here to a nearby cafe. We'll talk quietly there. - He suggested, hoping Amy hadn't noticed how his body was reacting to her. Immediately, however, he felt that was impossible. She looked at him with her big eyes as if she didn't know what to ask him.
- Good. - Rzekla kept his sanity. They both rose from their chairs and left Ralph's office.

Moments later, Amy and Ralph were sitting at a table in front of a coffee shop that was located next to the publishing house. Although it was slowly approaching eleven o'clock, the day was quite hot. The two sat facing each other. Ralph had his black glasses on, through which he was carefully looking at Amy. He wore the glasses on purpose because he didn't want to give away how much he admired her cheekbones, eyes, and lips. Amy sensed that a strange atmosphere had been born between them because Ralph didn't say anything but looked as if in front of him.

She decided to wait until the awkward silence passed. At that moment, a waitress approached them with coffee. The girl immediately smiled at Ralph which Amy noticed. She thought that probably Ralph must come here often. There was already coffee on the table, so it was easier to focus on something else. Amy took a sip when she suddenly heard Ralph's voice.

- Let me address you by your first name, you also call me Ralph. Amy looked with slight trepidation at the man sitting across from her. She was a tad surprised by this.

- In these circles, it's easier to cooperate just like that. - He chuckled roughly. Amy only bit her lip and nodded to him.

-Sure. I understand. - She said calmly. Ralph sighed and shook his head. He clearly wanted to get the conversation with the girl over with.

- Okay, let me put it another way. Amy stuck her gaze on him.

- I don't want you to misunderstand me Amy, but try to see me as your friend. Every literary agent Is the author's best friend. When working on a book, you spend a lot of time together. You authors may not realize it, but we are trying to help you.

-Is that really all this is about? - Asked a somewhat reassured Amy. - Yes. - Ralph stated. A gentle smile appeared on Amy's face. It was evident that she was beginning to feel more at ease in the company of Ralph, who also noticed this.

He averted his eyes and for a moment seemed as if he was thinking. Then he took off his glasses and looked at Amy again.

-Until now we have never published books by such young authors before. - He began in an uncertain voice. Amy was beginning to wonder what he was trying to tell her.

-Your book is a classic detective story combined with romance. We have always rejected all such innovations.

-Then why did you decide to publish my book? - She asked full of the tension she was now beginning to feel in her body.

- It is well-written, in addition to sensing freshness. Today's readers are still looking for something new, and you can give it to them. - Ralph stated in a slight reverie. Amy breathed a sigh of relief at this point. She was already worried for a while that the publication of her book was not so certain.

- Do you think my book will sell well? - She asked what she was so worried about. Ralph leaned toward her.

- I think... - He began to polish his words very slowly.

- That is a year you will make a lot of money from it.... - He added with a smile on his face.

CHAPTER 1

Amy once Davis and now for a year Jones spent every evening almost the same way. She reviewed notes of her ideas with her computer turned on, where she wrote something down every now and then. She even enjoyed the lonely evenings when she could write on her computer in peace. A year ago she published her first book about a woman who went missing a week ago. Her neighbor hired a private detective to find her. The missing woman's dog was whimpering terribly behind the wall, and she couldn't watch in peace her favorite TV series, which was airing on Filmbox after 8 pm. And so this missing woman fell in love with a man who, although he did not know her and had never seen her before, relentlessly searched for her. After finishing the book, Amy immediately thought to herself that although it was a detective story, the title "The Detective and the Missing" fit the story perfectly. All in all, you could say of her novel that it's a romantic story. Completely different from her marriage. A year ago she agreed to marry her literary agent Ralph Jones, who has now become co-owner of the publishing house Empire Books right after her debut.

From the very beginning, each of them knew that this was not a heartbreak or a burst of desire but an investment for the future. They are united by work and only work. They can do whatever they want and don't have to explain themselves to each other and use their freedom as they, please. Perennial is one paragraph in their marriage contract. She can devote herself completely to her work, while he leads his life, which is why Ralph is often away from home.

Of course, except for official receptions, during which

have to pretend to be a loving married couple. The only benefit for Amy is that she doesn't have to rent a modest apartment as she did before only apartments in a beautiful, large house in a quiet Chicago neighborhood. Amy always imagined that someday she would meet true love and fall in love rather than marry out of convenience, but after a few months of marriage, she concluded that this is more convenient after all. Since she became a famous writer she can devote herself only to what she has always dreamed of. That is, to write. She had already been sitting at her computer for three hours, tapping her fingers on the keyboards of her new laptop, which she had received as a gift for her twenty-seventh birthday from her husband. The most romantic gift Ralph could afford. Although she was much more fond of the diamond earrings she had accidentally found in his jacket pocket when she took the dirty clothes to the laundry. Maybe for a moment she hoped that the earrings would turn out to be a birthday present for her, but that didn't happen either. She felt a slight disappointment when she was given a laptop as a gift, which she is now so adamant about not parting with. She had been writing for quite a long time in the living room where she so enjoyed working. She always claimed that this was where she could focus best until her neck went numb. She tried to straighten up and licked her dry lips. She looked at the mug that stood next to the computer and immediately felt thirsty. She lifted the mug to her hand, but it was already empty. She got up from the computer and ran to the kitchen. She turned on the kettle and reached into the cabinet that was hung above the kitchen. She felt like making herself a cup of tea
when she suddenly heard a text message signal that someone had just sent it to her phone. She closed her locker and looked back. She glanced

On the phone, which was lying on the table behind her. She walked over and read the message.

- We'll be right there. - It was a message from her friend Cora. She went through all the messages quickly and displayed an earlier text message from her as well.

- In 30 minutes we'll drop by with Jackson. Be ready. Cora. Amy just sighed heavily after reading the message.

- Oh. Does she really have to come in today? - She asked herself but immediately looked at her watch. She knew that Cora and Jackson would probably be here soon, and she was so unprepared.

She was wearing a plain white T-shirt and black leggings. She reached for a glass of water that stood on the table. She took a sip. She set the glass down and ran upstairs to her bedroom with the phone in her hand. Entering her room, she turned on the light, threw the phone on the bed, and opened the closet. She didn't know how she should dress.

- Cora will probably wear something elegant again. - Amy thought.

- Ever since she married an Australian banker she always dresses so refined. I guess I should follow her example. - She added quietly as she looked through her closet. She immediately pulled out a little black from her closet. She quickly changed into a dress that hugged her hips tightly and made her breasts visible. She took time to gather her dark hair and put it up in a loose bun.

She then walked over to the mirror that hung opposite the bed. She swiped twice on her lips with pink lipstick, which perfectly highlighted her gray-blue eyes. Leaving the room, she put on black stilettos, turned off the light, and left the room. Walking to the first floor, she already heard the doorbell ring.

- But this Cora is so punctual. - She added. She cast a glance around the living room. She quickly turned off the computer and gathered her notes. Everything
She tucked into the dresser that stood by the door. The doorbell rang again. Amy opened the door and saw her blonde-haired friend Cora in a short red dress and a leather black couture with a bottle of wine she held in her hand.
Upon seeing her guests, she sent them a warm smile.
-Jackson and I decided to drop in on you. Happy birthday. - Cora chuckled. Amy glanced at the man standing next to the woman.
Hi. - She threw in a greeting. - Hi. - Jackson replied. - Enter the living room. - She added letting the guests in.
- Are you alone? - Cora asked, sitting down on the sofa.
- Yes. Ralph has a lot of things to do since the publisher appointed him as his deputy - Amy admitted trying to hide her confusion.
- Sure. - Responded Cora letting her friend know that she guesses that this is not the first evening she probably spends alone. - I'll open the wine. - He interjected
Jackson. - Good thought. You have to celebrate Amy's birthday, which was that week. - I'll take you to the kitchen.

Meanwhile, Ralph Jones was pacing nervously through the dark room, where the light from the bedside lamp standing on the dresser was softly burning. All the while, Ralph was being watched by a slender blond-haired woman to whom the men were paying attention. Bella Smith had been his mistress for a long time. One of many with whom Ralph had been dating, but this acquaintance had lasted almost five months. Bella sat comfortably in an armchair and ate slices of pizza, seeing

Ralph's nervousness she wiped her mouth with a napkin and approached him. She tried to gently put her hand on
his shoulder, but Ralph, who previously stood with his back turned to her, suddenly turned around.
-Do you really not want to try the pizza? - She asked in a calm voice. Ralph only sighed heavily.
- Listen. I have to tell you something. - He began. - Yes? - She asked more seductively.
- Everything is over between us. - He confessed at last. Bella looked at him in disbelief. - What do you mean? Are you still angry with me that I called you at home that week and your wife answered? - She asked after a while, regret could be heard in her voice.
- No matter. You shouldn't do it, but it's hard already. My decision has nothing to do with it. - He added and reached into the pocket of his jacket and took out the brown box of earrings that Amy had previously liked so much.
- This is to say goodbye. - He said. He reached for Bella's hand and closed the gift in her grasp. - Forgive me. - He added at the end and headed for the exit. Bella looked away and looked with eyes full of tears at Ralph leaving her apartment. As soon as she heard the sound of the door closing behind the man. She immediately burst out crying.
She glanced at the nicely wrapped box that Ralph had left for her then turned around
in the right direction and threw the box against the wall with all her strength. Out of it fell diamond earrings on the floor, which gently glittered in the dim light.
- What an asshole. - She shouted after the man hoping Ralph would hear her, but he had already managed to leave her apartment. He walked quickly across the parking lot and got

into his car. Before starting the engine, he reached for his phone, which was resting on the
The bottom of his pocket. He dialed his home number and put the camera to his ear. He waited for the call.

Hearing the phone ring, Amy looked away and looked where the sound was coming from. For a moment she hoped that maybe it was Ralph calling, but she immediately came to her senses. - Why would he call his own house? - She thought. She wanted to get up from the sofa. In one hand she held the glass of wine that Cora had brought today, while Jackson held her other hand. Cora, meanwhile, was bustling around the kitchen preparing snacks.
- Amy - She was snapped out of these thoughts by Jackson's voice. Despite her will, she had to look at Jackson. He was sitting in the chair in front of her and still did not let her hand out of his hand.
-You know. I have some ideas about your cover design. - Started Jackson trying to get his attention.
- I know, after all, you are a talented graphic designer otherwise Ralph would not have accepted you. - Said Amy slightly confused by Jackson's sudden interest. At that moment Cora entered the living room with a tray of snacks and, as if nothing had happened, squeezed past them pretending not to notice anything.
- Well, we already have sandwiches. We can continue celebrating. - She stated in a firm tone sending both of them a smile.
- Here's to Amy, so that her next birthday will be even more joyful. - Jackson, who was watching her closely, spoke up. - To Amy. - Cora repeated. Then the sound of the doorbell rang. Amy breathed a sigh of relief.

- Surely your husband is back? - Cora commented with slight displeasure. - Ralph never rings the doorbell. - Amy declared, then got up from the sofa. On the table
She set down her glass and went to open the door. To her surprise, Lucas Brown, the head of the publishing house, Ralph's partner, where Amy also publishes, stood in the doorway. The man looked to be in his fifties, dressed in a gray suit. He smiled at her in greeting.
- Hi. - Lucas chuckled. - Hi. - Responded Amy, a little confused by the publisher's visit.
- Is there a Ralph? - Ask Lucas.
- He is not at home at the moment. - Admitted Amy stammering a little. - Strange we had an appointment. We were supposed to talk about new contracts today.
- I don't know anything. - Amy assured him.-
Sure. Can I come in? - Of course. - Casts Amy letting the man through the door. Lucas immediately headed into the living room and looked around the room. It was clear that he was a little surprised by what he found in Ralph's house.
Cora took a big sip of wine until she felt sick.
She felt that the unannounced visitor was watching her closely. She grunted and set her glass down on the coffee table. She corrected her hair, which she tossed behind her back in one sweeping motion, and sat down more comfortably on the sofa. She looked with an impenetrable expression in her eyes at Amy's publisher, almost with the same look that Lucas Brown was looking at her with.
-Mhm. - Cora spoke up, who tried to break the uncomfortable moment of silence.
- I see that you are indeed very busy.... - Commented the blonde-haired woman in a poised tone while exhaling the words very slowly. Lucas' cheeks became hot at this moment as if he

was ashamed of this small suggestion. Immediately, however, composure came to him.
- As you can see. I deal with things constantly. - He replied coolly. Amy and Jackson listened to this exchange of words. Both understood little of it. However, it occurred to Amy that her friend must have met her publisher once before, but she could not recall under what circumstances it might have been. She was convinced that the two knew each other although they tried not to let it be known. Finally, Amy decided to speak up first.
- I didn't know you two knew each other. - She remarked stammeringly. In doing so, she glanced once at Cora and once at Lucas. After these words, Lucas felt even more embarrassed than moments ago,
and red bumps appeared on Cora's cheeks. However, she hoped everyone would think they were caused by too much wine. She looked away to avoid looking at her friend, who was standing next to her publisher.
- You don't remember Amy... - Cora spoke up, wandering her eyes around the living room.
- You once took me to a publishing house when we were shopping together. And then you introduced me to Mr. Brown. Amy considered her friend's words for a moment. She wondered if it really could have been like that. In her mind, she searched for those memories. Finally, she remembered that Cora was right. While working on the publication of her first book, a certain
At once she and Cora went shopping together. They walked around the stores all day and browsed through clothes. Amy was looking for the perfect outfit for her first interview, which she was to give for the Chicago News, and Cora helped her. After

spending many hours in the stores, Amy finally managed to buy an ecru-colored dress. The whole thing was made of lace. When they both felt so tired they went to a nearby cafe for coffee. They only had time to rest for a while when Amy's phone rang. Lucas asked that Amy suddenly come to the publishing house, he wanted to discuss something important with her. Amy suggested that Cora, who got married two weeks ago, go with her to Empire Books. Delighted with the prospect of Cora getting to know what it's like to work at the publishing house, she immediately agreed. And that's when Amy actually introduced Cora to Lucas. She almost didn't remember it anymore.

Lucas, after greeting them, immediately led Amy to the graphic designer and left immediately himself. Amy even had the impression for a moment that Lucas liked her friend. But she immediately thought that it was just an illusion, after all, Cora has been happily married for two weeks. Sometime later, Cora admittedly questioned Amy about Lucas, but she thought her friend was probably just plain curious. Amy snapped out of these thoughts when she finally heard Jackson's voice.

-Amy. - Called out once again the man. Amy felt that by her silence all eyes were on her. She felt uncomfortable. She smiled at them.

- You guys are right. I almost forgot that I once introduced you to each other. - She replied calmly in deep thought. Cora breathed a sigh of relief as did Lucas, who looked around the living room. - I see the party is going on at its best. - Threw Lucas suddenly trying to change the subject, looking closely at Jackson and Cora.

- We are celebrating Amy's birthday, which was that week. - In a firm tone, Cora replied without looking away

From a friend's publisher. Lucas turned toward Amy, who was standing behind him.
- Why don't you see if Ralph left those contracts for me somewhere? - Ask.
- Sure. Let's go to his office. - Amy suggested and set off.

Entering Ralph's office, Amy turned on the light in the room. She felt a little strange here. She rarely visited her husband in the office, and now in front of Lucas, she didn't want to come off as a wife who knows nothing about her husband's work. With a stab of slight trepidation, she approached the desk that faced the door. She glanced at the papers that lay on the desk, hoping that she might find something here. Lucas slowly approached in her direction. - And what? - Asked after a while.
- I don't know, I don't see anything here, I don't even know what I'm looking for. - Amy replied, forcing a smile on her face.
-Can I take a look around? - Asked Lucas uncertainly.
- Maybe I can find something before Ralph comes?
-Sure. - Responded Amy after a moment's thought, although she wasn't sure if she was doing the right thing by letting the publisher rummage through her husband's documents. She wasn't sure if Ralph would mind. Suddenly, a gentle smile appeared on Lucas' face.
- I'll be in the living room if you need anything. - She added heading for the exit. Lucas looked behind her as Amy was already closing the study door.

Ralph parked the car in the driveway. He took the keys out of the ignition and turned off the radio in the car. All the way to Home wondered what Amy was doing. He was surprised that she didn't answer his phone or call him. He looked away and looked at the house. His expression was puzzled, to say the least, by the fact that the lights were on throughout the house. For a moment he wondered why the house was so lit up. It was unlike Amy. Whenever she worked in the living room she always turned off the lights everywhere and turned on a tiny lamp that only illuminated her screen. He got out of the car and walked across the street. After a while, he was already on the grounds of his mansion. He walked up to the door and was about to pull the handle when he noticed a box wrapped in decorative paper lying next to the door. He leaned over and picked up the box, which he examined carefully. At first glance, it didn't seem suspicious. Finally, he noticed a sticky note on the box with a strange inscription - Last *Birthday.* He thought for a moment, it was a strange inscription. The box was not signed. Curious about the contents inside, Ralph opened the box and noticed that there were only papers inside - newspaper clippings. Ralph immediately thought that someone had played a nasty prank on him and Amy. He closed the box again and thought it best to get rid of it right away. He turned around and walked over to a trash can that stood nearby. He threw the tossed box in the trash and entered the house.

Cora took a sip of red wine. She moved the glass away from her lips, which she then looked at. She was silent for a moment then sighed. She reached for the bottle of wine and poured herself another glass.
- Ah... - She finally spoke up to the man sitting across from her.
- Pass me a glass Amy - She suggested.
-Why don't you wait for her with the wine? - Jackson suggested.
- No need, she should cheer up
- Why do you say that? Does he have any problems?
- You see nothing. Her marriage is a total failure.

-How can you know that? - Jackson wondered, reaching for the ham sandwiches.
- She's a friend of mine. I can see that there is something to it. - Commented Cora while taking a big sip of wine.
-Do you think Ralph doesn't love her? Cora looked at Jackson with a grim expression on her face.
- After all, it is everyone knows that the marriage of Amy and Ralph is just pure business. - She cast a firm tone. Jackson nearly choked on a bite of his sandwich after Cora's words.
-Calmly," Cora chuckled as she heard Amy approaching them.
- And how was it? - Cora asked, glancing at her friend who sat down next to her. - On-time.
-We added more wine for you. - Jackson spoke up, handing the glass to Amy. He completely didn't understand why but tried to touch the top of her hand with his fingers. - Thanks. - Said Amy with calmness written on her face. Jackson hoped that Cora didn't notice how much he was trying to get closer to the woman sitting across from him. Amy took a sip of wine, and at this point, she wasn't sure if she had a prediction or if Ralph was really standing in the hallway leaning against the doorframe. She watched the man for a moment. Suddenly he moved from his seat. - Ralph. - She called out to Amy, not sure if she was doing the right thing, but it was the only thing on her mind. At that moment, all eyes from the living room were directed in front of the
man. Ralph sent his wife a warm smile, which gently appeared on his face.
- Hello," Cora spoke up, and Jackson just nodded.
- Hello Coro. - Ralph replied, but not out of friendship but rather out of politeness.
- I see that when I am not at home you are well ? - He chuckled groggily as if he was trying to suggest to his wife that he was

not happy with what he found in the living room when he returned home. Amy immediately understood his suggestion. She didn't know why, but it made her sad. She looked at Ralph with sadness in her eyes.

-They did. Cora and Jackson just stopped by. I'm not going to suggest you join us because a guest is waiting for you in the study. - She replied with a slight regret in Amy's voice and immediately had the feeling that she regretted those words.

-Who came? - Ask Ralph hoping nothing bad came up from Bella.

- Lucas. Apparently, he needs some documents from you.

- She added. Ralph sort of breathed a sigh of relief.

- I'll check what it's about. Have fun," he chuckled as he walked away and headed toward the living room exit.

CHAPTER 2

- Hi, Ralph threw, closing the door behind him. Lucas was looking through documents from a large red binder and turned around when he heard his partner's voice.

-Hi. - Responsible Lucas turned his attention to Ralph but immediately returned to reviewing the documents. Suddenly He shook his head as if something had happened that he didn't like. - It seems to me that we had an appointment? - Asked in a dry tone. - Forgive me. - Ralph suddenly said, walking closer to the desk. - I had to run some errands in town. - He sighed heavily. - Sure. - Lucas nodded as if he didn't believe his partner's words.

-Did you find the contracts? - Ralph asked. - Yes. Thanks. I'll deal with these documents tomorrow. - Ralph. - Lucas suddenly called out.

-Let's talk better about Amy's contract. I think she should start promoting the book as soon as possible. - Threw without warning Lucas, who carefully watched his partner's reaction. Ralph only smiled under his breath and began to gently shake his head.

-You know it is still in the process of being written.

- This will only bolster sales of her new book. Ralph will be pure profit. We will make more money on her.

-She doesn't like to be distracted. - Ralph tried to convince him. Lucas suddenly threw the document binder on the desk. A loud bang could be heard throughout the office. Ralph, who was surprised by his partner's reaction, looked at him but said nothing.

- Forgive me. - Said Lucas, who was ashamed of his reaction. He put both hands on his hips. - Talk to her. She's your wife I'm sure you'll be able to convince her somehow. - He commented. Ralph fixed his gaze on the man standing across from him. He swallowed with difficulty strong. It was as if his friend's last words had caused him pain.

Amy escorted Cora and Jackson to the door. She seemed depressed, or perhaps she was more worried about Ralph's reaction, who apparently didn't like that he found her in the company of her friends. She was a little embarrassed by Cora and Jackson. After all, Cora never liked him anyway. She had always thought that dealing with Ralph was the last thing she should decide to do, but Amy was quite different sentences. Ralph's presence always helped her when meeting with readers.

- Do you really want us to leave already? Let us know, then we'll stay and help you clean up, right Jackson? - Assured Cora turning once to Amy and once to Jackson believing that the man would surely agree with her opinion.

- Of course. - Jackson nodded. Amy just smiled but didn't want to say whether she liked Cora's idea. - Thanks, but you'd better go. And so Ralph has already returned, I think he's not in the best mood.

- Your husband's moods do not concern us. - Rzekla dryly Cora.

- I know," assured Amy, glancing at her friend with an investigative eye. Cora sensed that they would be better off leaving Amy alone now.

-In that case, hang in there. - Threw in a changeable tone Cora and kissed Amy on the cheek. Jackson tried to do the same, but he held back at the last moment. He felt the whole situation a little confused.

- See you tomorrow? - He asked suddenly.

- Of course, it is.

- At noon?

- Perfect. - In that case, it's until tomorrow. - He said on his way out
And went outside. Amy closed the door behind him. Outside, Cora started looking in her tiny purse for cigarettes. She pulled one out and quickly lit it.
Jackson looked at the women, who at that very moment began to look at him
- I think it's a good start. - Threw in Cora suddenly.
- I don't understand. - Jackson wondered. Cora only smiled with satisfaction. - Is that so? - She asked as she walked past the man. A confused Jackson watched as the woman approached the car.

After Cora and Jackson left, Amy went to the living room. She started to collect the dirty dishes on a silver tray and carried everything to the kitchen. She already felt tired. She felt like leaving it all and running quickly to her bedroom, but she still had Ralph's expression in front of her. His cold stare did not give her peace of mind. Therefore, she decided that with the rest of her strength, she would clean up the dishes after the party she unexpectedly had to prepare for Cora and Jackson. She started washing the dishes in the sink. At first, she wanted to turn on the dishwasher, but after a while, she thought it was pointless. Her fatigue was becoming more and more apparent that she didn't even hear Ralph, accompanied by Lucas, leave the office. Ralph still turned off the light in the empty room and was immediately back next to his waiting partner. It seemed to him that Lucas wanted to tell him something else. His expression in his eyes clearly indicated that.
- Ralph. - Cast Lucas suddenly, although the publisher's eyes were clearly wandering somewhere.
- Yes?

- You know that the situation is not certain in publishing. We have to do something to stay in the market. Ralph listened carefully to his partner's confessions. He only nodded his head giving a sign that he agreed with him.
- It's not just about publishing your wife's book, but also about other publications. - Added Brown as Ralph continued to remain silent.
- Lucas, please don't mention to Amy that the publication of her book may be in jeopardy. - Ralph finally spoke up. Lucas sighed heavily.
- Well, I will not say. - Assure him, Brown. - But something must be decided. The men's voices quieted when they both heard the clatter of dishes coming from the kitchen. Ralph looked out over Lucas' shoulder with his eyes. He noticed that Amy was still hanging around between the living room and the kitchen, cleaning up after the party. He guessed that probably Cora and Jackson had already left.
-Let's keep our voices down, Amy is nearby. - Ralph suggested.
-Bright.
-What do you want to do? Do you have any ideas, Lucas? - Asked a slightly irritated Ralph as he walked past his partner, then stood behind him. Lucas suddenly turned toward Ralph's back.
-I hope I manage to settle what I've been running after like this for four days. - Commented Lucas looking intently at Ralph, who by this time had managed to lean his left hand against the doorframe. He stood almost motionless and watched implicitly as Amy cleaned the living room.
Suddenly Lucas walked closer to Ralph.
He lightly patted him on the shoulder after which Ralph looked at his friend.

- I'll let you know once I know something. - Brown added. Ralph nodded his head.

- I'll walk you to the door. - Ralph offered, and the two men headed for the exit. On the way, you could still hear their quiet conversations, which quickly quieted down. Amy thought the publisher must have left. She only realized this when she heard the sound of the door closing.

Immediately Ralph appeared in the kitchen. Amy, feeling his gaze on her, turned in his direction and looked at her husband.

-Has Lucas left yet? - She asked to break the silence.

- Yes, just now. - Ralph replied, put his hands in his pockets, and took a few steps toward her.

- How did the meeting go? Did everything go well?

-She asked, trying to sense the reaction if her husband was angry with her for letting the publisher into the office in his absence.

-Bottom line. What he was looking for he found. - He stated indifferently. Amy continued to wonder if Ralph would say anything else.

- Isn't it better to set the dirty dishes in the dishwasher?" he asked so suddenly which Amy didn't expect.

- She broke down. - She replied in a calm tone while unscrewing the water plug.

- Yes? Why didn't you say anything?

- I said, but you were in a hurry.

- Well, I will take care of it tomorrow. - Ralph assured her. Amy was still waiting for some reaction from her husband. She could clearly see that Ralph was worried about something. She tried to follow Ralph's steps with her eyes so that he wouldn't notice when he approached her from the other side.

-Did you have a good time with Cora and Jackson? - Ask in a poised tone so that it is difficult for her to sense what really drove him now.

- Good. - Amy commented. - I didn't know you knew Jackson so well. - Ralph tried to drone on.

- More Cora than me. They live in the same neighborhood. I Jackson met the publisher. - She admitted.

- An interesting coincidence. - Reflected Ralph glancing in the direction of the window.

- Possibly. Maybe I'll get to know him better when he gets here tomorrow. - She admitted.

- Is Jackson still coming here? - Ralph was suddenly puzzled, looking closely at his wife, who continued to wash the dishes and paid no attention to him.

- Yes, he is supposed to show me some cover designs for my book. I thought you knew. - She said without conviction.

- Of course, it is. That's a great idea. - He replied by walking closer to Amy, who was trying with all her might to fix her eyes on the dirty dishes. Finally, he took the plate she had just washed from her, gently mussing her fingers. It was at this moment that Amy felt a strange shiver on her skin. Ralph pulled the washcloth that lay there off the countertop. He began to wipe the plate while gently glancing at his wife, who continued to do the dishes.

- Amy - Ralph tried to speak up.

- I would like to talk to you about something. - He finished in a shy tone. Amy drew in a deep breath turning her gaze back to her husband.

- Ralph - She began in a pleading tone. - Please just not today. Let's talk tomorrow. I'm really tired already.

Ralph smiled through clenched teeth, but it was not what he wanted to hear now. - Okay. Amy turned off the water stopper and headed toward the kitchen exit. Behind her followed Ralph,

Who turned off the light? The two climbed the stairs to the first floor, then each went to their bedroom.

CHAPTER 3

Amy couldn't get to sleep all night. Too many things kept her awake. She wondered if Ralph couldn't sleep either and, like her, rolled from side to side. The moments until dawn appeared were anguish for her. As soon as she saw light coming through the window she immediately got up from her bed and ran to her bathroom. She quickly changed into blue jeans and a loose white blouse. She put on delicate makeup and went down to the first floor. As she descended the stairs, she had the impression that the house was very quiet. She immediately thought that probably Ralph wasn't up yet. In the kitchen, she began to tussle and prepare breakfast. She poured herself a cup of coffee and, putting the kettle down on the stove, reflexively looked at the clock that hung next to the window. Indicate that it had just passed seven-thirty. It was at this moment that Amy realized that it was not as early as she thought. So she must have fallen asleep in the morning, and the clock in her bedroom must have run out of batteries. She was already convinced that she would probably see Ralph in the kitchen soon. She set a plate on the table with the jam and omelets she had managed to fry that morning. And also the bacon snacks that her husband liked so much. Sitting down opposite the door, she suddenly spotted Ralph in front of her, who seemed to look very elegant. His dark shirt added a certain mysteriousness to his appearance, and the black pants he was wearing further emphasized his exposed figure.

- Good morning Amy. - Ralph began by sitting down across from her.

- Good morning. - Amy replied, wondering why her husband had assumed such a formal volume.

- How did you burn? - Ask suddenly while spreading butter on his bread. Amy immediately thought that he probably asked this question out of politeness, because what could he care. She took a bite of the omelet she had previously spread with peach jam before answering him.
- Well. - She admitted after a while, forcing a gentle smile on her face. She was afraid to start getting red in the cheeks because of an innocent lie. - And you? - She asked the same way.
Ralph's gaze suddenly fixed on Amy. For a moment he wondered what to answer. He was clearly puzzled by the question.
- Also good. - To state laconically. While sipping his coffee, he kept a close eye on his wife.
- Amy - He began in a serious tone setting the cups down on the saucer.
- Yes? - She asked without paying attention to her husband.
-I would like us to become a real marriage. - He admitted after a while waiting for her reaction, who gently smiled under her breath.
- Well ... we are after all. - She stated as if she did not understand what Ralph really meant.
- That's not the point. I would like us to consummate the marriage. - He dared to utter these words after a moment's hesitation. Amy suddenly put the cutlery down on the plate and fixed a frightened gaze on her husband.
- What? - She asked in a concerned voice.
- I would like us to consummate the marriage. - Ralph repeated. Amy still could not believe what she had just heard. The man, seeing that the shock from Amy's face was not going away, suddenly pushed back his chair and squatted next to her, so that he involuntarily smelled her perfume.

- Amy. - Called Ralph touching the top of his wife's hand.
- I have thought about it very well. We are already married and I think we can really become a real family.
- But... what has happened to you so suddenly? - She managed to spout a still-shocked Amy looking away.
- I just want to... - Ralph tried to say, but suddenly he didn't know what words he should use. His attention was focused on Amy's soft lips. He immediately began to wonder what they might taste like. He remembered well the day they got married. It wasn't a very romantic wedding, as they had both decided only to have a ceremony in an office, but they were both very serious about it. Ralph remembers well that it was a warm summer day. Amy, despite Ralph's prejudices, arrived in a cab together with Sarah, who was to be her best man on the day. All because Cora, together with her husband, had to fly to Sydney and it could not be postponed. Ralph and Amy didn't want to wait any longer for the wedding either, so in the end, Amy decided to ask Sarah to be her maid of honor. She had always been nice and friendly to her, so immediately Ralph's secretary agreed. She was even very happy about it. Ralph, who had previously arrived at the wedding palaces, stood outside accompanied by Lucas, who was to be his best man. However, for a while Lucas moved away to smoke a cigarette, so Ralph was left alone. He glanced at his watch from time to time, as if he was worried about whether Amy would definitely
has not given up on marriage. A week ago, they met with lawyers in his office, who handed both of them the premarital agreement that she and Ralph were to sign.
Up until the ceremony itself, Ralph wondered if Amy would protest and say that she didn't like something about the deal, but she was noticeably silent. Ralph slowly began to believe that she probably liked all the terms in it. It surprised him a little, but

he didn't want to exert anything on her. He preferred to wait for her to tell him herself. In the end, he convinced himself that it was probably okay with Amy for the two of them not to be faithful. Immediately, however, he thought about whether Amy would want to exercise this freedom right after the wedding. In spirit, he hoped that Amy would turn out to be a faithful wife after all, and he immediately realized that, after all, he hadn't talked to her about what their life together should look like later on except for living together. He also didn't believe that he would be able to last a lifetime and not touch any woman, but in the end, if Amy gave all of herself away to him then maybe she one would be enough for him for the rest of his life.

He was going to bring up the subject either before the ceremony or right after it. He looked at his watch again and at that moment a cab arrived from which Sarah got out

and Amy. At the sight of his fiancée, Ralph's heart beat harder. Amy indeed looked beautiful that day. Ralph walked up to her. To greet Sarah, who also looked spectacular that day. Ralph took Amy's hand and sent her a warm smile, which she also reciprocated. Sarah, seeing her boss and Amy, moved away from them so they could talk casually for a while.

- Amy, I'm so glad you're here already. - Admitted Ralph in a warm tone. Amy suddenly furrowed her eyebrows.

- Were you afraid that I was going to go awry? - She asked, guessing his fears. Ralph only nodded.

- After all, you still could. - Replied a focused Ralph at Amy's gaze.

- Don't worry, I didn't make up my mind. - Amy admitted.

- That's good. - Ralph took a breath and took a red box out of his pocket.

- I did not have the opportunity to give it to you before. - He said, opening the box that contained the diamond ring.

- Ralph. - Amy called out. - This is unnecessary.
- I think otherwise. - He admitted and slipped the ring, which fit perfectly, onto Amy's fingers. Amy looked at Ralph, who also reciprocated her gaze.
- Amy. - Ralph called out suddenly. She sensed that the man's tone had cooled noticeably.
- I wanted to talk to you. - He started when Sarah, accompanied by Lucas, suddenly approached them.
- We have to go inside already. - The bridesmaid castles.
Tension appeared on Ralph's face. He took Amy's hand and led her into the wedding palaces. He watched her carefully throughout the ceremony. He kept wondering how he managed to get her to marry him. Certainly, Amy was not desperate. Maybe the recent events had slightly dismayed her, he sensed that her decision was only taken from the fear she felt. However, that was not important now. The most important thing was that she would soon become his wife and they would become a married couple. That was all that mattered now. Once they had signed the documents and the clerk officially announced that they were married Ralph wondered if Amy would let him kiss her. He didn't know if he could allow himself to make such a bold gesture.
Although it occurred to him that now he didn't have to to ask her permission, but he immediately thought he shouldn't do anything until he had a serious talk with her. He was afraid that Amy might have been offended by this, and he didn't want to lose her friendship. So he figured it would be safer if he only earned a gallant gesture on his part. He kissed her hand, then allowed himself a subtle kiss on the cheek.
Although Amy looked gorgeous in a pale pink dress, which was gently flared from the waist. Small roses were woven into her dark hair, which perfectly emphasized her delicacy. He

wondered if Amy was offended by this, but preferred not to place a kiss on her lips until he had discussed it with her himself. Between his musings, all he heard was applause and congratulations to the clerk and Lucas and Sarah, who began to wish them well. Ralph involuntarily turned in their direction. He only noticed how Sarah wished the two of them good luck on their new path in life. He had a feeling that his secretary really wanted to be a good friend to Amy. Lucas patted Ralph on the shoulder and also wished him luck.

Suddenly Ralph returned to those memories as if he wanted to experience it again. And again he thought of his wife's lips. He felt like kissing her so hard when suddenly. they both heard Ralph's phone signal. The whole beautiful moment flew away somewhere.

Ralph woke up and took his hand away from Amy's hand. With a heavy sigh, he pulled the phone from his pants pocket.

-Yes? - He asked. Amy listened to the conversation, but her thoughts were still wandering somewhere. All she could think about was what Ralph had just told her. She wasn't quite sure if he had said it seriously, maybe he was just joking. However, more

She was terrified at the thought that he could kiss her, and she could return the kiss to him. In the end, there was even more confusion in her thoughts. - After all, Ralph has a lover. - Her thoughts began to call to her. - How could he propose to her? Did he want to have both of them? After all, she could never agree to such an insult. And why did it cause her pain? Or maybe his lover was calling him now, and she was listening in. - Good. I'll come right away. - Threw Ralph suddenly and disentangled himself. Amy didn't know if she should look at her husband.

- Forgive me. - He confessed and pushed back his chair. For a moment he seemed nervous. In an instant, he became completely different.
- I have to run an urgent errand. - He added and left the kitchen.
- Sure. - Amy replied, but Ralph was not visible. However, she said it more to herself.

Ralph quickly left the house. It seemed that the phone call that rang in the morning must have made him very nervous. Without looking back he got into his car and sped off. He didn't even realize that the man who had parked the car across the street from his house was watching him the whole time. As soon as Ralph wasn't seen around, the man got out of the car. It was Jackson. He quickly rushed to Amy's house, who was still sitting in the kitchen absorbed in thought. The doorbell rang to wake her from these musings. She got up and went to open the door. For a moment she thought that Ralph must have forgotten something. She didn't expect to see Jackson at the door so early.
- Hi Amy. - Jackson called out, sending her a smile.
- Hi. - Amy replied.
- You look like you're surprised. - Jackson chuckled suddenly.
- I didn't expect you so early. We only had an appointment for noon, right? - She stated with a slight indignation in her voice.
- Sure enough. I thought I'd stop by your place earlier, I just happened to pass your husband as he was leaving.
- Well. - Amy tried to reassure herself.
- So what? Can I come in? - Jackson tried to sound shy.
- Okay, come on in. - Said Amy, letting Jackson inside.

CHAPTER 4

Back in the living room, Amy turned on her laptop. Jackson sat down across from her. He looked around the interior as if it was the first time he had been in the room but his attention was still drawn to the woman who stood next to him. Feeling Jackson's gaze on her, Amy chuckled lightly.

- Wait, I'll make coffee. - She said and went to the kitchen. Jackson led her away with his eyes. After a while, Amy came into the living room again. She held two coffee mugs in her hands. She handed one to Jackson and set the other next to her. By this time, Jackson had already managed to connect a flash drive to Amy's laptop.

- I'll show you some projects, maybe you'll like something. - He admitted with a slight smile on his face. Amy reached for her coffee mug and took a sip. She tried to focus however her thoughts kept wandering around Ralph's words. - Sure enough. Amy

She waited patiently while Jackson began checking files. With one eye from under the computer he watched her, she seemed nervous.

- Amy - Jackson began suddenly. The woman's gaze fixed on the man.

- What is it about? Not feeling well, do you want to postpone it? - Asked Jackson with concern in her voice. Amy just shook her head.

- Ah. - She sighed. - It's all right. - She lowered her gaze to the hands that rested on her thighs. Jackson scooted his chair closer to Amy and in an instant placed his hands on her palms.

- Amy, tell me what's going on? How can I help you? You know I would do. - Jackson tried to confess. Amy unexpectedly took her hands away, feeling too close to the man.

Jackson fell silent.

- Show these graphics, maybe, some of them will be suitable for covers. - Amy spoke up, trying to change the subject. Jackson moved the laptop to his side and began opening the files in the folder one by one.

Suddenly, the phone that was lying on the dresser rang. Amy got up from the table and answered the call.

- Yes, I'm listening. - Amy spoke up. Jackson tried not to listen to the conversation but heard only what Amy was saying into the earpiece.

- How so? But now? - Amy was surprised.

- Good. - She said finally and disconnected the call. She immediately put the phone to her chest and took a deeper breath.

Jackson turned toward Amy.

- Is something wrong? Any bad news? - Ask. Amy put the phone on the forks.

- Ralph called. He said you urgently need to return to the publishing house. - Said Amy slowly. She was clearly shocked by her husband's sudden phone call. She turned to face Jackson and leaned her body against the dresser.

- Apparently, Ralph and Lucas are waiting for you. - She said in a calm tone, although Jackson could clearly see that she was nervous. He just didn't know what more. With the fact that Ralph had called or perhaps that their meeting together had been interrupted in such a way. Jackson turned away from Amy, unhooked the flash drive from her laptop, and stood up from the table. He looked again at Amy, who did not move.

- Good. - He said in a whisper so that she could barely hear him. - I'll check what it's about. We'll finish next time. Amy just nodded. After a moment, she heard the door behind Jackson close.

The evening seemed very peaceful to Amy. She made herself a cup of warm tea and returned to the living room. She sat down on the couch and opened the books where she had last finished reading. She tried to focus on the passage she was reading but struggled to focus her attention on anything. A gentle breeze flowed into the living room through the slightly ajar terrace door. It was helping Amy relax a bit if not for the thought of being alone in the house waiting for Ralph. The whole house was filled with a blissful silence that echoed throughout the interior. Suddenly Amy heard some strange rustling coming from the garden. For a moment she thought a flower pot that stood on the terrace had fallen over. Amy looked away from the book and directed her gaze to the terrace door, but in this darkness, she could not
notice anything. She closed the books she had placed on the sofa in one motion and stood up. She walked to the terrace door with her heart beating hard and tried to look outside.
She had the impression that for a moment she smelled some strange, foreign odor, but when she took another look at the garden, where leaves were gently beginning to move on the trees, she decided to let it go. She decided that maybe it was the wind that had broken for a while after all
And her overactive imagination probably worked. She closed the terrace door and sat down on the sofa. She reached for her books while watching the terrace door carefully. For a few more moments, she still had the illusory hope that a figure might appear to her, but she slowly averted her eyes and started

reading the books again where she had last left off. Fortunately, the next few moments passed quietly. Half an hour later, she heard the door open. She recognized from the footsteps and the smell in the air that Ralph had returned home. He walked into the living room, and although Amy didn't want to, she looked at him. For a moment she thought the expression in his eyes was different from that at breakfast, but she immediately chased those thoughts away. She concluded that Ralph was probably tired after a long day.

- I didn't think writers read anything else besides their books. - He chuckled blithely as if trying to relieve the mounting tension. Amy fidgeted slightly, closed the book, and threw it next to her.

- As you can see, sometimes it happens. - Rzekla rising from the couch. Ralph looked at his wife. She stood facing him while keeping her distance. He immediately felt the chill that beat her gaze.

-Was Jackson really so necessary in publishing? - She asked in a chilling tone. On Ralph's face appeared

He quipped, then turned his back to her. He headed to the bar, which was next to the entrance to the living room. He took out a glass and poured himself a whiskey.

- Do you want something to drink, too? - Ask by capping a bottle of alcohol.

- No, thank you. - Castles Amy, watching her husband. Ralph turned to her and realized that Amy was still waiting for an answer.

- What do you think? - Ask by drinking alcohol.

- Well, I don't know. - Amy stated with irony.

- He is a graphic designer. We need him all the time at the publishing house, there is always something to do. - He added while pacing around the room.

Amy crossed her arms over her shoulders.

- Is the cover design for my book also a matter for the publisher, by any chance? - She asked with a lame voice. Ralph's gaze lingered on his wife, who had idly lowered her hands from her shoulders.
- Of course, you will. Next time, have Jackson email you the designs.
- This will make contact much more difficult. It's just easier to agree on something this way. - She tried to convince Amy. Ralph just waved his hand, then took a few steps forward and set the whiskey glass on the table.
- Let's leave it, we should talk about more important matters for us. - He suggested with a gentle glint in his gaze. Amy sighed heavily.
- About what? - She wondered aloud. Ralph walked closer to Amy. - About what we talked about at breakfast.
- I don't think there is anything to talk about.
- But I think otherwise. I was serious this morning, I want us to be a real married couple from now on. Amy wondered how to fend off Ralph's attack.
- I don't really understand what it would look like? Ralph only smiled crookedly under his breath.
- What do you mean? We will become a real marriage, but not for show anymore, as it was before. We will make love to each other, sleep in the same bed and spend time together. If you want we can also decide to have children, but I'll leave those decisions to you. - Confessed Ralph is convinced of the soundness of his proposal.
- Really? This is a great plan. - She tried to mock Amy with her husband's idea. Ralph combed his fingers through his hair.
- There is no point in pretending that our marriage is more than a contract. - She accused Amy nervously. For the first time,

Ralph saw his wife's determination. In his mind, he wondered how to tell his wife what he felt in his heart.

But maybe tonight is not the best idea to confess his feelings. With a little disappointment, he turned his back on her and walked out onto the terrace. He looked around at his surroundings. There was darkness everywhere. Only the silence bothered him even more. He turned his gaze away from the empty space where the grass was overgrown. On the right side of the terrace, he sat down in an armchair on which a maroon pillow lay. He lowered his gaze to the floor.

Suddenly he heard the footsteps of Amy approaching him, who stopped as soon as he crossed the threshold. Ralph unwillingly looked at his wife.

- And why do you think so? - He asked. Amy felt offended that Ralph could not understand her concerns.

- Because something is missing from this idea.

- Like what? - Asked and at the same time looked away from her. Amy took two steps toward her husband trying to maintain her composure.

-Maybe just feelings. - She admitted in a calm tone.

- Feelings? - Ask Ralph as if he could not believe what he had just heard from his wife's mouth. - For example. - Amy confirmed.

- Feelings can be shown in many ways. - Communicated Ralph rising from his chair. He walked over to Amy and took her by the arm. For a moment she had the feeling that he might be about to kiss her, and she wouldn't be able to resist it.

She knew that this would completely betray what emotions she was stirring up. She was convinced that it was about to happen when she suddenly noticed that there was a change in Ralph's gaze. -

Let's go inside the house, it's getting chilly. - State

With a composed tone. Lead her back into the living room. He slid the terrace door behind him then walked over to the table and picked up a glass of undrinkable whiskey, which he stared at for a moment. Amy stood motionless against the wall.

- What about Ms. Bella Smith, then? - She continued to stop by Amy. Ralph set his glass down on the table as if he had already been discouraged from drinking the whiskey to the end and looked at his wife with a more understanding gaze. He made it clear that he didn't understand what Amy might be going on about.

- What role do you envision for her in our marriage? - I don't understand what you are asking. - Cast Ralph looking away from his wife.

- I know you are having an affair. - Who told you that? - He asked as if with remorse and looked away.

- No one had to. I guessed. Besides, after all, I mentioned to you before that she called here some time ago.

No, of course, I don't hold a grudge, that's what our agreement was after all, that each of us can do what we want. What I don't understand is why do you want to change the terms of our agreement? - Amy asked. Ralph swallowed his saliva with difficulty. Turning his gaze

In the direction of his wife, he noticed single tears running down her cheek. He wanted to go up to her and hug her tightly but with his remaining strength, he restrained himself.

- It's a done deal. - He admitted and in one moment wanted to ask her forgiveness, but at the very thought of the terms of their premarital agreement, he concluded that it was unnecessary after all.

- Ah yes... - sighed heavily Amy as if every word Ralph said made her feel even more pain. She suddenly pressed her lips tighter together which Ralph noticed.

- I see that each of us insists on our own.
- Don't expect anything else. - She stated firmly. A mocking smile appeared on Ralph's face.
- I think you will quickly change your mind. We will become the kind of married couple we should have been from the moment we got married.

Amy was lying in bed, it was the middle of the night. She still couldn't fall asleep, turning from side to side as if the bed she always sleeps on was not comfortable. In her mind, she started counting down the time until dawn, but she immediately felt sick as soon as she thought that tomorrow morning she would have to face Ralph again. Suddenly she thought about why she had agreed to marry Ralph. She knew from the beginning that it would only be a business deal. She was also aware of this, that Ralph would have no affection for her, and yet she agreed to marry him. And immediately the memories of a year ago came back to her. Yes, it was that fear.

After the author meeting in the bookstore was over, Amy began packing a notebook in her purse, which was on the table, as well as a bottle of water and the pen she always used to sign books to readers. The bookstore seemed empty, the last reader having left 20 minutes ago. Amy, who was already feeling tired, was also getting ready to leave. She didn't even notice that for those 20 minutes, she wasn't alone. One man stayed in the bookstore and surreptitiously watched her, who, before she closed her bags, still took out a mirror
From the powder room to touch up her makeup. The man, taking advantage of Amy's inattention, approached her quietly. He placed his hand on Amy's shoulder, who, feeling a stranger's touch, became frightened. She rapturously turned toward the

man. At the sight of Amy, the stranger only smiled widely showing his teeth. It seemed to Amy that he was not yet forty years old. He was wearing worn worn blue jeans and a black T-shirt.

- Please do not be afraid. - The man began. Amy tried to calm down.

- I wanted her to sign books for me. - He gestured and handed her the books, which Amy hadn't noticed before. - Good. - Whispered Amy trying to remain calm. She took the books from him and noticed that she had probably already managed to hide her favorite pen, which she always used to sign copies with. So she opened her bags and with one hand tried to find the pen, but it was nowhere to be found.

Suddenly a stranger

The man took out his pen and handed it to Amy, who involuntarily looked at the man. She stopped looking in her purse for her pen.

- Please sign books for me with this. - The stranger spoke up showing his teeth. Amy took a deeper breath as if to feel relief. She nodded and took the pen from him.

- What is your name? - She asked in a poised tone.

- What? - The man was suddenly surprised. Amy glanced at the stranger.

- For whom should I sign books? - She tried to explain.

- Ah. yes. - The man breathed.

- Have the lady sign for Carter MacDonald. - Explained the stranger in a cheerful tone.

- Good. - She nodded to Amy and made the dedication. She put a pen inside and handed the books to the man. The stranger looked at the signature the writer had made. Taking advantage of the stranger's inattention, Amy quickly reached for her bags and turned to leave. She was already right at the door when suddenly a man approached her. He grabbed her by the shoulders and turned her toward him.

He then pinned her against the wall and rubbed his stubble against Amy's delicate cheek. It was a disgusting sensation for her, and she smelled an odor that made her sick.

- Please don't touch me. - She shouted. The unfamiliar man apparently this threat only angered her even more, he was already about to embrace her breast when at that moment Amy forcefully brandished a powerful kick at his crotch, after which the assailant immediately scowled. Amy ran quickly out of the bookstore. Without turning back she ran all the way to the front of the

herself on her high black stilettos. She hoped to be at the hotel, which was not far from the bookstore, soon. She ran into the hotel out of breath, but there was no one at the reception desk. All the time she had the impression of a stranger's gaze on her body, but she did not find enough courage to turn around behind her. Without waiting for the elevator, she ran up the stairs to the second floor. The corridor was empty. With a quick movement, she reached for the card in her purse, which she used to open the hotel room door. She rushed quickly into the room, turned the door lock behind her, and leaned with her back against the door. Closing her eyes, she mentally began counting to ten to calm her nerves. Slowly she felt the tension draining from her. Suddenly she noticed someone slowly pressing on the door handle. At that moment she felt all the fear return to her, through which she could not make a sound. Then she heard someone tugging on the doorknob with all his strength. He starts banging on the door as if trying to break it down.

Amy, who didn't know how to react, put her hand over her mouth to prevent any sound from coming out. Tears began to appear in her eyes when she heard some unintelligible cursing.

She became so frightened that she involuntarily slumped to the floor. And then she heard some other male voice.

- What are you doing here? Do you have a room booked here? - The voice came from outside the door. She thought it was probably the hotel's security guard. After a moment, both voices fell silent. Amy felt she could finally start crying. She took her phone out of her purse and dialed Ralph's number, who quickly answered her call.

- Ralph, can you come to my hotel? I'm afraid to be here alone. - She howled through her tears then hung up and cried even louder.

Then she didn't remember it very well as it happened that moments later she was sitting on her bed drinking a glass of water. In front of her room door stood one of the hotel's security guards. At the time, Amy was accompanied by one of the receptionists who kept her company and a friendly doctor who also had a hotel stay booked. At the express request of the staff, they assisted Amy, who still seemed shaken. While she was trying to calm her nerves at the time Ralph, who was deeply concerned about the whole situation, rushed into her room like a storm. Immediately after Amy's phone call, he called the hotel manager, who recounted the events to him. He didn't wait a moment longer but immediately returned to the hotel to check how Amy was feeling. Upon seeing Ralph, Amy fixed her gaze on him.

Fear and pain were evident in her eyes, which somehow stirred something in him.

He saw her pained face as well as her pallor. This madman must have seriously frightened her. Immediately after Ralph, a security guard rushed into the room and failed to stop Ralph.

- Who are you? - The doctor was outraged. A frightened man in his seventies. - You broke into the room. - Commented the

security guard, who was standing behind Ralph. He had the distinct urge to forcibly lead the posh man out of the room. After the bodyguard's words, Ralph turned to him over his shoulder and looked at the man in uniform.
- Calmly. - A slightly stunned Amy spoke up.
- Please don't throw him out. It's not his fault. - She protested. Ralph looked away again and looked at Amy. He approached to her and knelt by her legs. He looked at her with a caring gaze.
-Amy, how do you feel? - Ask.
- It's okay now. - She admitted. - I didn't need to bother you.
- I think otherwise, it's good that you called. - She was interrupted by Ralph keeping calm.
- I shouldn't leave you alone. - He added after a while. The doctor's grunting sounded in the room.
- Can you explain to us your intrusion into the room? - The older man spoke up in a more forceful tone. Ralph turned toward the doctor and the bodyguard over his shoulder then stood up and approached the men.
- Of course, sorry. My name is Ralph Jones. I recently learned about the whole incident.
- Who are you to this lady? - Ask the security guard with a glance at Amy.
- I am... I am... - Ralph tried to explain, suddenly swallowing his saliva with difficulty.
- Fiancé. - He answered in such a way that Amy couldn't hear him speak.
- Ah. - The doctor sighed. - It's okay. I gave your fiancée medication to calm her down, please don't leave her alone. She is very upset.
- Of course. - Ralph nodded to him. The security guard's gaze also softened.

And then Amy woke up from those memories. She lay in her bed again and was safe. This was the only reason she had agreed to marry Ralph, she now knew for sure. She turned on her left side.

- I did all this just to feel safe. - She didn't even realize when she said those words out loud. She hid her face in her pillow and fell asleep.

CHAPTER 5

When Amy woke up in the morning she was glad that Ralph was not at home. Before she left her room she wondered how she should behave when she met her husband at breakfast. How good it was that Ralph made it easy for her and left for work before she got up. She walked into the kitchen and looked around. On the table was still freshly brewed coffee and a steel plate covered with a cloth with writing on a white sheet.
For my wife. Amy barely squirmed at this inscription. She knew that Ralph was not letting go any further, but she immediately thought about how much longer he would be able to pull this off. However, the answer flowed into her thoughts very quickly. Probably until he meets another beauty on his way. These musings confirmed her conviction that she could not give in to Ralph's persuasion. In one motion, she pulled the cloth off the plate and saw the breakfast prepared for her in front of her. Ralph seemed to have thought of everything. On the plate were delicacies she liked. There were nuts, bread with pumpkin seeds, a teaspoon of pineapple jam, and fried bacon. The whole thing looked very appetizing. She sat down on a chair and poured herself a ginger coffee. She began to slowly savor her breakfast and then thought to herself that Ralph must have worked hard. When she had time to take a sip of coffee then a phone signal sounded from the living room.
Amy thought it was probably Ralph calling. She decided not to to give him satisfaction and not answer the call. She hoped he would eventually hang up. The signal stopped ringing but the answering machine voice came on immediately. Amy wondered why Ralph would leave a message at the post office. With a strange feeling, she wiped her mouth with a napkin and got up

from the table. She went to the living room and stopped in front of the dresser on which the phone stood.
- Good morning, this is Commissioner Max Roy. He called you to confirm his concerns. We are assured that Mr. Carter MacDonald is at large. Please let your wife know in advance. Let's stay in constant contact. - She heard Amy, then a deafening silence fell. Amy froze after those words. MacDonald is on the loose. She felt again the same anxiety as a year ago, those terrible fears, Ralph's care, and concern.
And then she realized something. She was already sure why Ralph wanted them to be a loving couple. It was, she guessed, not out of love but out of a sense of fear. Again, her life is threatened by a psychofan, from whom she thought she had already managed to free herself. The truth, however, was quite different. Carter MacDonald is the man who tried to attack her in an empty bookstore, then followed her on the way to her hotel and tried to force his way into her room. Had it not been for the intervention of a security guard, there's no telling how it all might have ended. For a brief moment, Amy wanted to start deluding herself that Ralph had begun to feel something for her. However, as it turned out, it wasn't a surge of affection he just wanted to keep her safe. He was afraid that some madman might threaten her life, and then the publishing house would lose one of its better clients. Amy became sad, she didn't even know when one tear started to
run down her cheek. With a quick flick of her hand, she wiped it away to ward off these considerations.

That day Ralph left home early in the morning. He sensed that Amy might be in a bad mood after the last evening.
He decided it would be better for him to sneak out of the house quickly. He made an early morning appointment with Lucas at a

coffee shop in downtown Chicago. He had been sitting there for a good fifteen minutes and had already managed to eat breakfast. He also ordered coffee for himself. The waitress at the time handed him cups when Lucas approached the table.

- Hi Ralph. - He threw in a greeting.

- Hi. - Ralph replied with a slight sigh in his voice.

-It's the same for me, too. - Turned Lucas to the young waitress, who nodded and moved away from the men.

- How are you doing? You said you had some important business. - Ralph chuckled.

- Yes. - Responded Lucas intertwining his hands on the table.

- I managed to get invitations to a literary festival. - Lucas admitted. - You could go with Amy. - He suggested.

- Mhm, good thought. - Admitted Ralph.

- How did you manage to arrange it?

- I managed to persuade a woman who works at the cultural center to get our publishing house on the list. - Lucas admitted with satisfaction. Ralph took a sip of coffee after his partner's words.

- Do you mean to say that you slept with her in exchange for these invitations? - Ralph was clearly surprised.

- Well, no kidding. - Lucas replied. At this time, a waitress approached them and handed Lucas his coffee.

-Please. - The woman said. - Thank you. - replied Lucas glancing at the waitress. After which the two men were left alone. Ralph suddenly fell silent, which did not escape Lucas' attention, who looked at his friend for a moment.

-What's wrong with you, Ralph? - Lucas spoke up. Ralph breathed heavily.

- Nothing. - Jones tried to assure.

-After all, I can see, say.

- Commissioner Roy called me that McDonald had escaped from prison.
- What? - Lucas called out suddenly. Surprised, Ralph looked at Lucas.
- Does this mean that Amy is in danger of something?
- I hope not.
- What do you want to do? Have you told her?
- Not yet, but I will have to do it soon.
- Sure. What about the festival then? - Lucas asked uncertainly.
- All right, we'll go there together with Amy. - Assured Ralph, then looked at his watch.
- Sorry Lucas, but I have something else to take care of. I have to go now. - Rivers getting up from his chair.
- Sure. - He nodded, putting his hand over his mouth as if he was thinking. Ralph left the café. He didn't even notice that their conversation was being carefully listened to by a man sitting next to them at a neighboring table. He looked as if he was reading a newspaper, but as soon as Ralph left the café, he took his eyes off the newspaper and carefully watched Jones leave. After walking out into the street, Ralph inadvertently bumped into a woman who was just about to enter the cafe. At first, he didn't notice that this woman was his wife's friend.
- I apologize to you very much. - We heard back from Ralph.
- Nothing is wrong. - The woman replied. Ralph fixed his gaze on her.
- Ah... Cora is that you? What are you doing here? - Asked strong for politeness, who after these words smiled at him.
- I made an appointment here with a friend, maybe he is already waiting for me.
-She stated Cora maintained a kind of calmness, even though she was fuming with anxiety from inside. She didn't want Ralph to notice, and she was afraid that he would mention it to Amy.

- Sure. Sorry, I have to go now. - Responsible.
- Sure, go ahead. - He nodded at Cora, who watched carefully as Ralph got into his car
And she leaves. She only glanced through the glass still to the cafe
and noticed that Lucas was sitting at the table immersed in his thoughts. She turned to the door and went inside.

Amy turned on her computer in the living room. She felt bad that she had neglected her work a bit lately. All because of Ralph's proposals, which still did not give her peace of mind. Now she felt a little better because at least she knew Ralph's motives. She knew how she should prepare herself if he mentioned again how much he believed they could become a real family. On the one hand, she tried to focus on her work, while on the other, she glanced at the terrace with one eye. It was as if she was afraid that someone might barge in. She tried to chase the bad feeling away and then she felt someone's gaze on her body. She decided not to turn around and heard familiar footsteps.
She glanced at the man's figure. Ralph came home. He placed his left hand on her shoulder. Amy tried not to show how much she was trembling under his touch. She swallowed her saliva with difficulty
and tried harder to focus on her work. Ralph smiled crookedly. He kissed her on the top of her head and moved his hand
From his shoulder toward her back. Amy bit her lips and forcefully tried to straighten up. - Are you working? - She heard her husband's voice in a slightly seductive tone.
- Yes, I've been indulging myself a bit lately. - Amy admitted with remorse. Ralph took his hand from her and walked over. He pulled out a chair and sat right next to her. Amy looked at

Ralph and spoke up in a slightly frightened voice. - Are you going to sit here? - She asked. - And why not? - Ralph was surprised. - My presence shouldn't bother you. - He added. - You're the one who thinks so. - Amy commented.
She looked away from her husband and then looked at him again. His expression was implacable.
- All in all, it's good that you're already there. - She admitted.
Ralph felt a slight sneer in her statement.
- And yet. - He chuckled without taking his eyes off his wife.
- Mhm: We need to talk.
- I turn to listen. Amy looked at Ralph with a cold stare.
- I already know why you want to change the terms of our premarital agreement. - She chuckled with regret in Amy's voice.
- Yes? - Puzzled Ralph as if he didn't quite understand what she might mean.
- Yes, you are only concerned about my safety. You are afraid that if something happens to me then the publishing house will not earn anything from my
book. - She confessed while trying to hold back her nerves. Ralph leaned toward her.
- I don't think I understand. Can you explain more? - Ask while remaining calm.
- Don't pretend. - She called out Suddenly.
- Today a message was left on the answering machine by Commissioner Roy. He says that Carter MacDonald has escaped from prison. So it's all for that. - Shouted Amy pushing back her chair with a bang. She stood up abruptly unable to hold back her tears any longer. Ralph looked at his wife with an expression of amazement. In an instant, he wondered why Amy could come to such a conclusion. And immediately he came to his senses. He heard her quiet sobbing, got up, and tried to approach her.

- Don't even try to deny it. - She growled and turned toward the stairs, where she quickly found herself.
- Amy. - She heard him call out.
- Wait. - Ralph, who was already standing at the first step of the stairs, called out.
- I don't know why you thought that, but know that with all my heart I will try to keep you safe. I won't let anything happen to you. - He confessed thus in his voice, hoping that this would calm Amy's nerves. One could sense concern in his words but at the moment everything he said was not what she wanted to hear. She stood motionless on the stairs for a while longer, holding onto the banister with one hand, then broke off and ran even faster up to the floor. Ralph, sensing that he had done something wrong again, looked away from the staircase where Amy had been standing just a moment ago and combed his hands through his hair.

CHAPTER 6

Amy did not know at what point yesterday she fell asleep right after covering herself with a blanket. She seemed to be still reflecting on the events of yesterday's conversation
With Ralph. She couldn't believe it when she discovered his real reasons so quickly. Although it was already morning she still had a light sleep. Suddenly she was roused from this safe state of bliss by someone's conversations coming from the garden, which came into her room through a tilted window. Amy opened her eyes and looked around the room. In one involuntary movement, she averted her gaze and looked toward the window. She slowly sat down on the bed and after a moment got up. She put on her silk robe and walked to the window, through which she then looked out. In the garden, she spotted two young and rather heavily muscled men making themselves comfortable on Ralph's property. She was frightened. She wasn't sure what these men were doing in the garden. At first, she wanted to call out to them from the window, but immediately thought that was pointless. She backed away from the window
And she left her bedroom. She walked down the stairs to the first floor looking around the house. She wondered where Ralph might be now. He was probably in the kitchen at this early hour, but it was clear from a distance that no one was there. From the hall, she spotted him picking up the mail from the letter carrier. She wanted to approach Ralph but suddenly stopped halfway. She realized that she was not completely dressed after all. Ralph, meanwhile, managed to say goodbye to the mailman and close the door. Amy waited for him in the living room. Ralph, browsing through the mail on the way, immediately found himself facing Amy. Not

Looking at his wife, he immediately sensed her delicate scent. In one motion, he captured her gaze.

- Amy. - He called out to his wife, who had an impenetrable expression on her face. He immediately sensed her nervousness.
- Who are the men in the garden? - She asked in a donkey-like tone. Ralph sighed heavily and shook his head. At first, he wanted to escape from his wife's gaze and also from talking to her, but he immediately decided that it was pointless after all. He would have to admit everything anyway. With an assumed calmness on his face, he looked at Amy.
- These are your bodyguards. I hired them. - He confessed with remorse in his voice. Amy just laughed under her breath in disbelief. She thought to herself how Ralph could have said nothing to her that he was going to hire her protection. And suddenly she felt very uncomfortable. She realized that Ralph had decided for her, and had not even tried to ask her opinion. This hurt her the most. - And you didn't say anything to me? - Amy was offended.
- I wanted to talk to you yesterday, but you didn't want to. - He replied in a calm tone of the kind he could manage. - I had to do something. - He admitted after a brief moment of silence more emphatically.
- Do you think that settles everything? - Shouted Amy suddenly.
- Probably not, but it's all for your safety. Amy began walking nervously around the living room. Amy. - Ralph called out.
- Amy. - He repeated when he realized that his wife was not responding. Suddenly he approached her with a quick step. He turned her toward him and grabbed her wrists. Amy stood still, both of them looking into each other's eyes.
- Amy. - He began to speak very softly. There was a gleam in Ralph's eyes that she had never noticed before.

- I will do everything to keep you safe. I will not let anything endanger you. After these words, Amy trembled which Ralph also felt. He thought that although she didn't trust him, she was no stranger to his touch and the words he spoke to her. Amy swallowed her saliva with difficulty and continued to stare at him in silence. Ralph continued after a while.
- We will implement as much caution and security in our lives as the situation demands. - He added and loosened her hands from his grasp. With one hand he brushed his fingers against her cheek, and with the other, he put his arms around her waist and pulled her close. He put his arms around her firmly, so that Amy could listen to the rhythm of his beating heart. And she still wondered if Ralph had told her all this just out of concern for her safety, or maybe he was showing some other feelings for her. Immediately, these considerations brought too much confusion to her mind. She decided to interrupt this pleasant moment and look at everything with common sense. She gathered her courage.
- Ralph. - She tried to start Amy when Ralph's hand gently stroked her back. His touch made her feel even more secure in his arms. But she knew she couldn't let those illusions take control of her.
- Is there anything else I should know about? - She asked in a cautious tone. Ralph, after her question, abruptly released her from his embrace and moved away from her. He looked straight into her eyes. Amy tried to read from his gaze what kind of feelings he might be displaying but she could read nothing from his eyes.
He suddenly looked away from her.
- Go to your bedroom and get dressed, strangers are hanging around the house. We'll have breakfast and then talk about everything over coffee. - To state in a tone as if he was giving

instructions to his employee. He withdrew from the living room and then went to his office. Amy stood motionless for a while as if the impression of her husband's words still could not leave her. She immediately realized that, after all, Ralph never asks for anything but says what he expects. She wanted to protest but immediately realized that it would be of no use because Ralph had already made up his mind. She glanced at her reflection in the mirror and realized that she was still wearing her nightgown And a bathrobe. With that, she had to agree that she should dress up. Especially since she felt a tad uncomfortable in such an outfit. She turned toward the stairs to the floor and obediently went to her bedroom to change.

Ralph struggled to get himself under control. Entering his office, he closed the door behind him. He didn't want Amy to see his nervousness, and it would happen if he stayed with her a while longer. It was a good thing he had picked up the letters from the mailman, because that way he had some excuse that could be used as an excuse. He shuffled quickly through his office and suddenly threw all the letters on his desk so that they all fell apart.
He put both hands on his hips, looked away, and sighed heavily. Suddenly his gaze was once again fixed on the letters.
He noticed that three of them were not addressed. He leaned over the desk to look at these envelopes more closely, then reached for the letters. He opened the first unaddressed envelope, in which he found nothing. The letter was empty. He was surprised at what
made empty envelopes without any contents inside. He then opened the second one, which was also empty. It gave him a guess. Why would someone go to all this trouble to send empty letters to him and Amy. It was suspicious, to say the least. He

then opened the third unaddressed envelope. At first glance, he was surprised to see that there was some sort of white card inside. He pulled it out from inside and turned it inside out to see what was written. At that moment, his gaze suddenly faded. The white piece of paper was strangely written on. It was nothing like the death notice that is placed in newspapers. However, the name of the deceased person disturbed him more. - Amy Jones. - He repeated in his mind twice. That was the name described in the column of the person who died. The date and place of burial, however, were not filled in. The whole situation began to worry Ralph even more. He knew that for anything in the world, he could not show it. In addition, he was horrified by the painted crosses on the notice. It was clear that someone had specifically inflicted the

The effort to paint the symbols. He looked away and fixed his gaze on the window. At first, he wondered if he should throw it all in the garbage, but immediately thought it would be better to show it all to Commissioner Roy. Maybe he could collect fingerprints and tell if Amy's former stalker might be behind it. He circled the desk around. He slid out a drawer and there stowed all the empty envelopes along with the dreaded notice. He slid the drawer closed, which he then locked. He took out the key, which he hid in a casket that stood to the left of the desk. He left

From the study.

Moments later, Amy came down to the first floor again. She was already dressed and delicately made up. Her denim short shorts and powder pink t-shirt only emphasized her vulnerability. She entered the kitchen, where the table was already set. The smell of freshly fried omelets could be smelled throughout the room. Ralph stood with his back turned to her as he poured boiling water into the tea cups.

At the sight of Amy, he looked over his shoulder at her.
- Sit down, breakfast is ready. - He said in a calm tone, completely different from the conversation he had moments ago in the living room. She sat down in the seat she always occupied. She sent Ralph a warm smile as he handed her a cup of tea. She glanced at his apron, which he had tied around his waist, and thought he looked a tad funny in it but decided not to tell him that. Ralph sat down across from her. Their breakfast passed in silence. Neither of them said anything to each other. When Ralph noticed that Amy had already finished eating he suddenly rose from his chair and began to collect the dishes. - Now let's have coffee in the living room. - He suggested while putting the dirty dishes in the sink. Amy already knew that this coffee was an excuse because they were about to have a conversation. Without a word, she stood up
She from her chair and left the kitchen. In the living room, she sat down on the couch and silently waited to see what Ralph had to tell her next
saying. After a while, Ralph appeared next to her placing two cups of coffee on the table, the aroma of which could be felt in the air. Amy woke up from her silence when Ralph sat down next to her. The two began drinking coffee at the same time. Amy continued to wait to see if Ralph would start a conversation with her, but when he didn't speak for a long time, she decided to speak first.
- What are we going to talk about? - She asked in a calm tone. Ralph moved nervously on the sofa. He took another sip of coffee.
- There are a few issues I would like to discuss with you. - He admitted.
- So go ahead. - Amy urged him.

- Lucas urged you to start promoting your new book already. Amy sighed heavily after these words.
- After all, you know that the book is not ready yet. - She stated while looking at her husband.
-I know, but it will help later in the sale.... - Whose idea is this?
- She called out nervously to Amy. Ralph set the coffee cups down on the table. Then he turned his gaze to Amy and put his arm around her hand, who tried not to pay attention to his touch. She was afraid that the slight tremor might betray her now.
- Please agree to at least a few meetings. - He suggested in a calm tone. Amy only shook her head, all the while looking for a way to postpone the premature promotion of the book to a later time, but nothing came to mind.
- Okay, and the other thing? - She asked trying to change the subject. She didn't want to think about how much she liked Ralph's touch, which seemed to be getting softer every moment especially when he stroked the top of her hand.
- The publisher has received an invitation to a literary festival. There are to be premieres of upcoming books. I thought we could go there together, in fact, we should. - He admitted with a gleam in his eye.
- Why do you think so? - She asked trying to divert her husband's attention and take her hand from his grasp, but then Ralph tightened his fingers more firmly on her hand without hurting her.
- It's simple Lucas and I got invitations with accompanying persons. I can't imagine that my wife could be missing next to me. Besides, you will see the new premieres yourself, maybe something will interest you. - He argued as if he knew that Amy would agree with his opinion anyway.
After a brief moment of silence, Amy conceded his point.

- Good. - She answered but immediately wondered why she was able to succumb so easily to his persuasion. This filled her with all sorts of fears, but she didn't want to think about it for now.
- The right decision. - State with satisfaction Ralph, then let go of his wife's embrace. He set her cups down on the table
And he moved closer to her. Amy wondered if he would try to kiss her. She knew that in that case, she would have to protest, but Ralph put his arms around her tenderly and kissed his head on the temple. This gesture allowed Amy to breathe a sigh of relief but she immediately felt sorry, but she didn't want to let it show.

CHAPTER 7

The next few days passed in complete peace for Amy, not even Ralph tried to engage in a conversation with her about their marriage. Amy breathed a sigh of relief but at least Ralph's behavior seemed suspicious. This evening there was to be a literary festival on the occasion of which Amy spent the entire morning shopping. After leaving the house, she felt a breath of freedom. She was about to call Cora but finally gave up. She sensed that her friend would not want to help her choose a creation. After a while,

she found herself in the heart of downtown Chicago, where the most expensive women's fashion boutiques were located. Looking at the dresses on display, Amy was convinced that she could completely relax, but she immediately realized that two bodyguards were walking behind her, whom Ralph had hired. This completely took away the joy that was already entering her. After a short while, she entered an upscale boutique with no customers. Behind the counter sat a fashionable red-haired girl. Amy immediately thought that she was probably a student and was supplementing her tuition, just like she was a few years ago. Upon seeing Amy, the saleswoman smiled at her and immediately approached her.

- How can I help you? - She asked.

- I am looking for an evening gown. Something elegant, yet formal at the same time. - She admitted with slight confusion to Amy, who was blundering around the store with her eyes.

- Of course, I will find something for you right away. - She told the saleswoman and disappeared from her sight, who at that time began to look at the dresses hanging on the hangers. At that time, the saleswoman appeared in the store with three creations.

- I have something special for you. - Announced the girl. After these words, Amy turned to face the saleswoman.
Seeing the three gowns on the hangers that the saleswoman had chosen for her, Amy was not convinced about any of the creations. Nevertheless, she decided to try on each one in turn. The first gown was an ankle-length, thin-strapped creation, all in beige. Attention was focused on the numerous sequins that extended from the neckline to the waist. It lay quite loose on Amy, which is why she didn't feel comfortable in it. The other was a cornflower-colored gown.
It buttoned at the back of the neck with a huge slit down to the torso with a bow of the same shade tied at the hips. Although the dress seemed quite elegant Amy felt it would not be the right choice for her. It was more suitable for a big New Year's Eve party than for a formal event. The final gown in black seemed to be the best choice for her. It was simple yet elegant, so in the end Amy decided on this choice. After a few hours, she left the boutique satisfied and returned home. She knew she had bought herself a creation that was perfect for such an occasion. It was a long, black evening gown of shiny material on thin straps with a large slit on one side at the thigh.
Of course, it was quite expensive, but Amy didn't care about that. Ralph offered to give her his bank card, which he kept in his office at home, for this purchase. With a little hesitation, Amy took the card from him and paid with it at the store.

Now she was standing in front of the mirror and was fixing her hair one last time in a bun, from which one strand had unexpectedly slipped out. Suddenly Amy looked at her watch and realized that it was already so late. She swiped some more lipstick across her lips and left her bedroom. Ralph was anxiously waiting for her just below the stairs. At the sight of his wife, he turned and looked at her. A look of delight appeared on his face. Amy's creation was perfect in every way, especially since it was able to accentuate her figure.

Amy walked slowly down the stairs in high-heeled stilettos. Her steps spread throughout the house. Ralph still did not utter a single

of a single word only looked carefully at his wife. He walked up to her and extended his hand toward her. Amy shook hands with him.

- You look beautiful. - He commented on her appearance with a short sentence as if no other words came to mind now.

- Thank you. - Amy nodded.

-Just don't know if this dress is suitable for such an event. Maybe it's too formal? - Pondered Amy as if she wasn't quite sure how she should dress.

- She is perfect and fits you perfectly. - Ralph assured her, but in his dreams, he was only thinking about how to get her out of it by exposing her beautiful body.

- Let's go. - Wake up at last, pulling Amy with him. In front of the house, a car together with a driver was already waiting for them. Amy hurriedly sat down, and Ralph immediately appeared next to her. The two decided to keep silent the entire trip in the car. She looked out the window admiring the lights of Chicago, which was heavily illuminated at night. After a while, they found themselves in front of the exclusive *Palerso* Hotel, in front of which a crowd of journalists was already camped out. Ralph got out of the car first and shook Amy's hand. Together they went inside, paying no attention to the flashbulbs that began to surround them.

They were greeted at the hotel by one of the festival organizers, who upon seeing Ralph immediately approached them. Amy tried not to let on that the interior design impressed her although

Ralph glanced at her now and then. The two of them walked to the second room, where the entire artistic world was located. Amy noticed that the festival organizer had unexpectedly left them, but she felt safe at Ralph's side. As soon as she turned her gaze to the surrounding guests it was from afar that she noticed an older man in an elegant suit who approached them he was heading. After a while, the man was already standing next to them and greeted Ralph warmly, and he sent her a warm smile. Amy thought the two men must know each other well.

- Hello Ralph, how nice of you to finally show up. - The man began, glancing at Amy, who was listening to their conversation.

- Hi Steve. I too am glad we can meet again. Meet my wife, Amy. - Threw with evident satisfaction Ralph embraced her around the waist and pulled her close. Amy, who until now had no idea that Ralph wanted to show off his young, beautiful, and talented wife to his business colleagues, did not know how she should react to her husband's behavior in the company of a stranger.

- Amy, darling. - Ralph spoke up, glancing at his wife, who was struggling to catch his words.

- Meet this is Steve, a good friend of mine. He runs a publishing house in London and came to Chicago, especially for this festival.

- Pleased to meet you, sir. - Spoke Amy barely out of her daze. She sensed exactly that Ralph would not soon let her out of his embrace.

-Amy is a writer. - Ralph spoke up with a gleam in his eye. Steve was clearly surprised by this.

- Yes? And what do you write?" he asked, inquiring into the truth.

- Criminals. - Responded to Amy trying to remain calm. At that time, the organizer of the festival, whom Amy and Ralph met when entering the hotel, appeared next to the man.
- Sorry Steve, can we ask you for a moment? - Ask. Steve glanced at the organizer with a penetrating gaze.
- Sure, I'm on my way. - He replied and immediately turned to Amy
and Ralph.
- Forgive me. - He replied and disappeared into the crowd. After Steve left, Amy took a deeper breath of air, which did not escape Ralph's attention. He glanced at his wife, sensing that Amy was displeased.
- What is it about? - Ralph asked. Amy opened her mouth but said nothing. She decided to remain silent when a waiter appeared next to them with a tray of champagne glasses. Ralph reached for one glass, then handed it to his wife. Amy took a sip when unexpectedly someone behind her back poked her so that Amy choked on the alcohol. After all the commotion, Ralph pulled a handkerchief from his jacket and began rubbing Amy's cleavage. Suddenly, a journalist with a camera stood next to them.
Neither Amy nor Ralph noticed that from the opposite direction, Steve was already approaching them, but seeing the journalist stopped
Halfway through and listened carefully.
- Ms. Amy Jones? Is it true that your stalker Carter McDonald is at large and threatening your life again? - A journalist's voice rang out. Everyone wants to know your opinion about McDonald's escape from prison, will you comment somehow on these rumors? - Finished the journalist and suddenly a flash from his camera flashed. Amy and Ralph were so shocked by the whole situation that they were not sitting down how they

should react. Suddenly Ralph pulled his wife closer to him as if
he wanted to protect her from the whole world. Only Amy
seemed to have heard everyone in the room over the journalist's
words, and now the gazes of the curious were focused on her.
She longed to get away from there as soon as possible
And find yourself far away from everything.

Amy was relieved as soon as she managed to cross the threshold
of the house with Ralph. She was shaken. Tears flowed of their
own accord
on her cheeks. The only thing she was most afraid of was just
that someone would pull out the events of a year ago that she
had tried so relentlessly to forget. The journalist's words were
enough for her to remember everything again. She wasn't sure
how Ralph managed to get her out of the party, the most
important thing was that she was already
Away from the whole scandal. Nor did it matter what might
happen tomorrow. All the way home she and Ralph were silent.
It wasn't until passing the first-floor hall that Amy felt she could
give vent to her emotions. She already wanted to go upstairs
when she suddenly heard Ralph's voice.
- Wait, I'll give you something that can help you. - Ralph
suggested. Amy hesitated for a moment whether she should turn
toward her husband, who was standing behind her back.
Suddenly, when she involuntarily glanced back over her
shoulder, she saw Ralph heading for the living room. He
approached the bar, and Amy at that time turned around and
watched her husband's silhouette. In one motion, she wiped
away the tears streaming down her face. Her eyes were red, and
her lips were swollen from crying and her makeup was smeared.
And at that moment Ralph turned to face her. His facial

expression depicted no emotion. He held a whiskey glass in his hand.
- Come. - He called out in a calm tone, but it did not sound like a request but a command. Amy took a deep breath and approached her husband. Ralph handed her a glass of whiskey. With trembling lips, Amy took a sip. Ralph did not take his eyes off his wife.
At one point, she felt Ralph begin to stroke her hair. This sensation was unfamiliar to her. On the one hand, it gave her pleasure, but on the other hand, it was a foreign sensation to her.
- Better? - Ralph asked when Amy finished drinking her whiskey. At that very moment, Ralph lowered his hand from her hair. Amy suddenly felt that she was beginning to miss his closeness and touch,
Who was able to calm her down so much? And immediately, however, she thought she didn't know how she managed to drink the beverage with a hint of bitterness.
She only nodded, conceding the point to Ralph, who took the glass from her and set it down on the bar. He looked at her again. - That's good. - Ralph commented. Amy felt clearly that her husband was watching her closely; this filled her with some apprehension. Again he reached out his hand toward her but this time he did not stroke her hair but touched her cheek. Amy felt a shudder. In her mind, she wondered how far Ralph could still go, as he began outlining her lips with his thumb. He placed his other hand on her waist and drew her toward him. Amy realized that she had probably never been this close to him before. And before she had time to finish her consideration Ralph placed a kiss on her lips. Doubts still swirled within Amy, she wasn't sure if she should submit to her husband's caress. But then with a seemingly gentle

and insignificant touch, Ralph's kiss became more passionate, possessive, and commanding. Ralph put his hand on her back, while with the other he began to embrace her breast when suddenly something awoke in Amy. With all her strength, she pushed her husband away from her.

- How can you? - She screamed out loud. She felt so unhappy. Ralph didn't know for a moment how to react to his wife's rejection.

- Amy, please. - Ralph tried to persuade her, but Amy had not the slightest intention of listening to her husband's explanation. She took a step back.

- You don't think I'll agree just like that after everything that happened today? - She burst out crying and turned away. However, she immediately ran upstairs to her bedroom. Ralph decided that he would not give up.

- Amy, wait. - He shouted after her but Amy had no intention of stopping. She ran breathlessly into her bedroom, where she hoped she could take refuge from the world. But she only had time to turn around and saw the door open. Standing in it was Ralph.

CHAPTER 8

- What do you want? Give me a break! - Cried Amy trying to hold back an outburst of despair. Ralph stood for a brief moment as if motionless. His expression was implacable. He took two steps toward her and suddenly Amy thought Ralph's gaze changed. His face was not so tense but she could read nothing from his eyes.

- Amy, please. Don't push me away, not like this. - Ralph spoke up, trying to maintain a kind of calm. Amy's eyes became glazed, she barely restrained herself from bursting out with real, deeply hidden emotions.

- Stop, just go out and leave me alone now.

- I can't leave you. I'm very anxious to make you feel better. Amy felt her legs give way under her. There was something in Ralph's words that made her heart begin to soften.

- I didn't know that journalist would be there. - Tried to correct Ralph when Amy started walking back and forth across her bedroom along the window.

- I guessed," she admitted with a slight sneer in her voice, glancing at her husband. Ralph, seeing her nervousness, came even closer to her. He grabbed her by the shoulders and turned her toward him. Whether willing or not, Amy had to look Ralph straight in the eye. She swallowed her saliva with difficulty. There was determination painted in his gaze, as well as a willingness that he was ready to risk everything.

- I would never expose you to such a nightmare. I care about taking care of you. - He said these words although it seemed that he wanted to add something else, but decided not to say anything more.

- Because I am your wife? - She asked with a breaking voice tears appearing in her eyes.

- Because you are the person I will always take care of. - He interrupted her as if he wanted to assure her at all costs that she could feel safe with him. And after these words he moved even closer to her, and drew her close, their foreheads touching.

Amy struggled to catch her breath. This moment helped each other to master each other. With Ralph's entrance, everything was determined. The inevitable had arrived. Ralph began to seek her lips, wanting to taste them and enjoy them. But all the time he was gripped by the fear that if he loosened the grip in which he held Amy so tightly, she might escape again. And he couldn't allow that to happen. At one point, he felt Amy begin to reciprocate his caress. This pleased him but he didn't want to betray it. Their kiss from the one in the hall was completely different. They both realized where they were and why. Ralph embraced Amy even tighter, hugging her close. His left hand involuntarily went to her waist and then Amy rested her palms on the

His torso. Through his shirt, she could feel his muscles tightening. Ralph began to unbutton her dress with his other hand. He felt that his dream had finally come true. For so long he had wanted Amy to let him get close. He wanted such a moment to last forever. Now that he had tasted her lips, the touch of her body, and heard her soft sigh, he could not let her out of his embrace. He slipped the gown off her shoulders, which fell to the floor with a soft rustling sound. Amy, remaining in just her underwear, did not feel embarrassed. She carefully watched Ralph's gaze, in which she saw his great desire. She wanted him to embrace her even tighter. She didn't have to say the words out loud, Ralph immediately guessed what Amy expected from him now. He took her in his arms and put her on the bed. He placed another kiss on her lips. Then her hair in a bun came loose and spilled over the silky pillow. Amy decided not only to take from Ralph what he wanted to give her, but she also wanted to give him more herself. After a while, they lay in a strong embrace entwined with each other. Amy did not yet want to admit to Ralph how important this moment was to her. Until now she could only dream of her husband's closeness, their marriage limited to friendly conversations. Today there was a breakthrough.

Amy felt for the first time what it was like to be the most important person in Ralph's life if only for a moment. Their future was still in big question. She wasn't sure if she could count on anything more, but she was also afraid to ask. Ralph had been enjoying Amy's body all night, who was now sleeping next to him.

First thing in the morning, he woke up lifting his head and looking around. He looked at Amy, who was still sleeping by his side. She looked so peaceful. Ralph leaned toward her.

He kissed Amy's cheek with his lips, who did not even move. There was some strange noise coming from outside the window which worried Ralph. He got out of bed completely naked, but he didn't care one bit. He went to the window and looked out through the curtain at what was going on around him. Suddenly his face became gloomy. Ralph noticed a crowd of journalists surrounding their house. He closed the window curtain again and turned around with his face pulled down. He walked past the bed and began to gather his clothes from the floor. As he was already putting on his pants, he suddenly glanced at his sleeping wife.

- Amy, wake up. - Ralph called out. Amy, who only after a while opened her eyes. For a moment she wondered where she was

and immediately thought if what happened yesterday was by any chance a dream. But she immediately realized that she was lying in bed completely devoid of clothes. She glanced with an expression of embarrassment at Ralph and noticed that her husband was already putting on shirts. Suddenly Ralph looked at her, and Amy didn't know where to hide her gaze.
- Get up, you need to get dressed quickly. - He mouthed these words completely indifferently as if what happened between them last night meant nothing to him. The doorbell sounded coming from the first floor. Ralph held his jacket and became motionless. It was something he had been dreading.
- I'll go open it, and you get up. - He chuckled groggily and left the bedroom. Amy felt like crying but decided to stop the tears flowing into her eyes. She covered herself with a white sheet and went to the bathroom. She dropped the garment she had covered herself with on the floor and stepped into the shower. She turned offwater plugs and only when she felt a large stream of water on her body did she allow herself moments of weakness.

CHAPTER 9

Ralph, out of all this nervousness, opened the door with a sweeping motion. His expression softened when he saw Lucas on the other side.

- Hi Ralph. - Chuckled Lucas carelessly.

- Hi. - Ralph replied to him in a calm tone.

- I can come in. I have a case.

- Sure. - Nodded Ralph, who made room at the threshold of the door for Lucas to step inside. Before he closed the door, however, he looked outside and noticed that the crowd of journalists was not receding at all, but rather more and more were appearing. The flashing lights flashed again before Ralph had time to slam the door. He stood for a moment as if trying to hold the handle and only then turned to face his accomplice.

- Let's go into the study. - Suggested Ralph, who barely kept his composure.

- Don't bother, I just stopped by for a moment.

- Okay, then tell me how did you manage to get past those hyenas camped outside the house? - Ralph asked while putting his hands in his pants pockets.

- I told them I was one of them. - Lucas giggled. Ralph only smiled under his breath.

- Did they believe it?

- This is not at all improbable. - There was a brief moment of silence, after which Ralph took his hands out of his pockets and looked closely at his partner.

- What brings you to me? - Ask Ralph impatiently.

- How does Amy feel? - Spoke to Lucas in a voice full of concern.

- I heard what happened yesterday at the festival. - He added while combing his hair with his fingers. Ralph only sighed heavily.
- Dude, you don't even know how sorry I am. - He added as if he felt guilty about the whole situation.
-Give it a rest.
- You may have already talked to Amy about book promotion.
- Lucas spoke up suddenly as if trying to change the topic of conversation.
- For now, I just mentioned it to her.
- And what will he agree to?
- Probably yes, but certainly not at the moment, for now, we have to wait. - Admitted Ralph walking nervously around the lobby. Lucas' face clouded over.
- This is understandable. What do you want to do now?
- We will leave with Amy for a few days, maybe then the whole situation will quiet down.
- Good idea. - Chuckled Lucas roughly.
- Let us know when you know where you are going to go. - He added heading toward the door.
- Sure. - Ralph nodded.
- Take care, Ralph.
- You also Lucas.
Ralph only managed to close the door behind Lucas and immediately began to wonder what he was really doing with his life. Outside the door, a crowd of journalists is camped out, and he wants to run away from here like a coward.
Immediately, however, he thought of Amy. Now after spending the night together, their relationship seemed even more complicated. On the one hand, he wanted to continually hold Amy in his embrace, to enjoy the warmth of her body, and on the other, he was afraid to look her in the eye. His musings were

suddenly interrupted when he heard her footsteps coming from the upstairs hallway. He decided that he would go to the study and get on with his work. It would be better if they didn't exchange a word with each other now, especially since he had been so judgmental to her immediately after waking up.
How would he look into her eyes now. With a quick step, he rushed to the study. Amy managed to get down to the first floor and heard the sound of the door closing. She figured Ralph would be working late now.He will probably try to avoid me now. - She thought out loud. She didn't know why these words caused her so much pain in her heart. After all, she could have guessed it. What else would she have hoped for. A man who, for the sake of business, proposed marriage to her. He had a taboo of mistresses from the very beginning, so how could she hope for affection on his part. He would not turn out to be faithful, and would not make an exception for her. She knew it would be better for her if she stopped thinking about it over and over again. She took another look around the empty living room and reluctantly went to the kitchen.

In the evening, Amy stood motionless in front of the terrace door. It was a warm, evening outside, and Amy continued to watch the crowd of journalists who still occupied most of the street. Ralph emerged from his office and paced through the living room on his way to the kitchen. Suddenly stop and He looked at a thoughtful Amy, who stood motionless. At first, he didn't know if he should approach her. They hadn't spoken to each other almost since the morning. After their night together, he wondered what her reaction might be. He didn't dare to approach her, embrace her and comfort her. He could only hope that Amy had not sensed his presence. He was almost

determined to return to his office when suddenly his wife's voice rang out
in the living room.
- Today I couldn't leave the house all day. And that was even worse than sitting locked up. - Admitted Amy in a calm tone. Ralph knew that he could not trivialize her words. He swallowed his saliva with difficulty and walked closer to her, but halfway stop. He watched her from a safe distance.
- I know it's a difficult situation, but things should calm down in a few days. - He tried to be as convincing as possible, although he didn't quite believe his own words.
- Sure, because eventually they will hit on a bigger affair and get interested in it? - Asked Amy, but she knew well the answer to her question.
- And until then, should we not leave the house? - She asked with an angry look in her eyes turning violently toward Ralph.
- We have to wait it out. - Ralph assures her.
-How much? - Cried Amy trying not to lose control of her nerves.
- I don't know exactly. - Tried to explain Ralph when Amy crookedly smiled under her breath. Seeing his wife's increasing nervousness, he walked closer to her.
- Amy, calm down. - He called out in a calm tone, embracing his wife's waist and hugging her tightly. Amy, smelling her husband's scent, felt safe for a moment. Only now was she beginning to understand the meaning of the words Ralph had spoken.
- We can leave here for a few days. To some beautiful place, away from all the noise. There, no one will bother us. - A red light went on in Amy's head.
- Will we be there alone, away from everyone? - She asked with a slight concern that Ralph could sense in her voice.

- No one will disturb us, because no one will know where we will go. There we will be able to think about everything in peace.
- You mean over what? - He was interrupted by Amy.
- Over our whole situation, over our marriage, over us. - He admitted while maintaining a kind of calm. Amy felt that Ralph was smiling under his breath as he uttered these words.
- Do you think this is a good idea? - She asked feeling further apprehension about being alone with Ralph. In the end, she concluded that after all, she is also alone with him here. Everything that could happen has already happened, so she probably isn't risking anything anymore. - She thought as Ralph hugged her tighter and tighter.
- I think this is a very good idea.
- Say yes to Amy. - He whispered directly into her ear.
- In that case, I agree. - She said these words after a short moment of silence. There were flashes in Ralph's eyes. Everything was heading the way he wanted it to. He put his arms around her neck and hid his face in her hair, smelling the distinct scent that so intensely stimulated his senses.

CHAPTER 10

The next day Ralph woke Amy early, who was still asleep in her bedroom. The previous evening she had wondered if Ralph would be willing to get close to her again, but he clearly showed no initiative. After an affectionate gesture of hugging, Ralph pulled away from her and suggested that it had gotten quite late and they should go to bed. The two went to their bedrooms and closed the door behind them. On the one hand, Amy was glad that Ralph wasn't trying to get close to her, and on the other hand, she was sorry.

She thought that probably Ralph got what he wanted. Perhaps she didn't seem more interesting to him. Perhaps he felt more comfortable around Mrs. Bella Smith. These musings kept Amy awake all night. She didn't even know at what point she fell asleep, it was probably very late. She had hoped to sleep a little longer when unexpectedly she still heard through her deep sleep some murmuring coming from her bedroom. However, she was too tired and still sleepy to open her eyes and check what was going on. Suddenly she felt someone's touch on her shoulder. It was quite a pleasant feeling and already very familiar. The smell that was in the air reminded her of Ralph's scent, but after all, he couldn't be here in the room, because why would he come. She thought she was probably just dreaming it.

- Amy, getting up. - Suddenly she heard in her half-sleep. She immediately thought that she was already starting to have auditory hallucinations, but again she felt someone's touch gently shaking her shoulder. She involuntarily opened her eyes and turned her head. She saw that she had not dreamed at all. Above her stood Ralph, already dressed in black pants and a gray shirt. He looked like he was going somewhere.

- Get up, we are about to leave. - He said in an unobjectionable tone. Amy only managed to hold back a yawn.

She looked at him with wide-open eyes, she had the impression that Ralph was not serious about it.

- What? - She finally managed to speak up.

- We are leaving, I mentioned it to you yesterday. - He repeated calmly. Amy sighed and corrected herself on the bed where she sat. Her gaze was still directed toward her husband.

- I thought you were just joking. - After Amy's words, a look of clear displeasure was painted on Ralph's face. He took a step back and looked even more down at her. For a while, they were silent and measured each other with their eyes, but immediately Amy could not stand the tension that was floating in the air. She looked at her watch, which indicated five past five in the morning.

Resigned, she looked at her husband.

- It's only five o'clock in the morning. - She called out when Ralph was already heading for the exit.

- This is the best time, almost everyone is still asleep. We'll be leaving in five minutes. - He said this the moment he was outside the threshold of the bedroom. Amy heard his last words already from the hallway. She didn't have the strength to get out of bed. She wanted to cover herself with a blanket and still sleep, but Ralph's tone clearly worried her. She barely got out of bed and went to the bathroom with sleepy eyes. After a while, she felt a little better, especially as she took a sobering shower. She quickly dressed in a summer dress, as the day promised to be quite warm from

the morning. She managed to pack a few of the most necessary

things into her travel bag, although she had no idea what clothes to take since Ralph hadn't said anything about where they were going. She took a slow step down to the first floor, where Ralph was already waiting for her. He seemed a little impatient. He walked back and forth. As Amy walked down the stairs she watched him carefully. Finally, when Amy was already a few stairs away from the first floor, Ralph turned and looked at her.
- Finally. - He said in a completely indifferent tone, to which Amy did not respond. He walked over and took the bag from her, then grabbed her hand and led her out of the house.

Ralph threw Amy's bag into the trunk next to his own, which he had managed to stow away yesterday, and they both got into the car. The entire trip passed in silence, neither of them daring to speak up. Fortunately, the day seemed so pleasant that the quietly turned-on radio helped focus their thoughts only on the music, which they both tried to listen to.
Amy felt herself getting hungry after a while. Not surprisingly, they left Chicago so quickly that she didn't even have time to drink coffee. However, she hoped that they would make a stop along the way, but it didn't even occur to Ralph. He was trying so hard to focus on the road that it was possible he didn't even hear her stomach burping. Amy, trying to relax, turned her head to the right side and tried to admire the changing surroundings. Now
Most of all, she wanted to get as far away as possible from Ralph, who was surreptitiously looking at her. She could clearly feel his gaze on her and thought that Ralph must have heard it, that how hungry she was. She closed her eyes and took a deeper breath to calm herself down. She realized that it had been about three hours since they left Chicago. After a moment, she opened her eyelids as they passed the town of Two Rivers. Clearly

something was giving her second thoughts. She glanced at Ralph, who already knew what she wanted to ask him but wasn't about to turn in her direction.

- Yes, you are right we are already there. - He replied in a voice in which one could sense a distinct note of satisfaction.

- We will be home soon. - He added in the same tone. More and more surprise was painted on Amy's face.

- Home? - Amy wondered aloud.

- Yes, I will explain everything to you later. - He replied by sending her a warm smile, which clearly suggested that Ralph must have planned the whole trip. Amy just wondered why he had chosen Two Rivers in particular, whether it had any meaning for him. Once in the beginning, she had mentioned to him that she would like to visit the city, but she doubted Ralph would remember that. - But first, we'll make a stop and have some breakfast, I guess you're hungry?

- Ask though he knew the truth. Amy did not hear the last sentence Ralph said. With a grim smile on her face, she gathered the courage to answer him.

- Of course, he did. Ralph only smiled but said nothing more himself.

Ralph then turned into one side alley and stop in front of one of the restaurants, which served not only lunch and dinner but also breakfast. It was only at this point that Amy woke up from her thoughts. She turned her eyes and looked

On Ralph, who had already been watching her closely for some time.

- Why did we stop here? - She asked as if she didn't remember admitting out loud that she was hungry.

- We left so early that even I didn't manage to eat anything in the morning. Here they have really good cuisine. - He added and turned away from Amy.

- Let's go. - He replied, opening the door. After a while, they entered the restaurant. Sitting at a table across from Ralph, Amy thought he was really right. The cuisine seemed really tasty, or maybe she was just so hungry that she didn't care what she ate anymore.

Right after breakfast, Ralph took Amy for a drive around the neighborhood, during which her anger at Ralph slowly began to pass. She even began to feel more at ease in the company of her husband. Especially since she liked the area very much. All the surrounding monuments and memorials caught her attention. At times she was so tired that she asked Ralph to stop by for coffee, which was also excellent.

Maybe the fresh air was making her finally able to breathe away unpleasant thoughts. Or maybe she could just really relax in such comfort. In the afternoon, Ralph took her to Lake Michigan, which stretched from Chicago itself.

But here at Two Rivers, the water seemed clearer, especially since they felt a gentle breeze all the time. Ralph took a blanket out of the trunk and spread it on the grass. Then he went back to the car to get the basket of food they had prepared for them at the restaurant. And he sat down on the blanket next to Amy, who didn't even think that Ralph could afford

to prepare such a romantic picnic by the lake. Now she began to get to know him from a completely different side. He seemed more interesting than a principled boss who thinks only of selling her book. Ralph sensed that Amy's thoughts were revolving around him. Unexpectedly, he moved even closer to her and brushed her lips with his mouth. Amy responded to his caress. Their gazes met again. They didn't look at each other the way they had this morning, but they were filled from within with a love they hadn't yet realized. She wanted to ask for more, but after a moment she pulled away from him. She still remembered well the chill he had bestowed on her after their first night together. She thought it would be better not to go back to that, and so she felt tired.

Ralph wondered what was going on with Amy, he didn't recognize her behavior. Suddenly he noticed that Amy was settling down on the blanket as if to sleep and closing her eyes. He thought she was probably tired.

He moved closer to her but Amy was already asleep. He looked at her once more and stroked her hair.

In the evening, Ralph's car stopped in front of a wooden house that was softly lit in the twilight. Amy blinked and looked around. For a moment she wondered exactly where the two of them were. It seemed to her that Ralph had probably booked a hotel, but she didn't think that they would be spending the next few days in such a charming cottage as it looked. Nor did she notice that Ralph had already gotten out of the car, walked around the car and opened Amy's door, and shook her hand.

- We are on the spot. - Rivers encouragingly. Amy shook his hand and got out of the car. After a while, they walked closer after

door. Ralph searched in his pocket for a moment for the keys. Just as he was turning the lock on the door, Amy couldn't stand it and spoke up.

- What is this place? - She asked in a calm tone still looking around. At this moment, Ralph managed to open the door.

- Let's go inside. - He suggested and let her through the door. Amy stepped inside but didn't manage to see much. The room was in total darkness. Ralph turned on the light and closed the door behind him. Only now Amy was able to look at the entire room. The interior seemed small, but very cozy. There was a

living room with a single bright sofa in the middle, a fireplace in front of it, and a small coffee table in the middle. Across from her, she spotted a door of some sort. She figured it was probably a bedroom door. The other one, unfortunately, was not there. She guessed that there was probably only one bedroom in such a small lake house. Next to the living room, she could see a table and chairs, probably the kitchen was there. And then there was the bathroom, somewhere it was probably located, but Amy at the moment did not see where it might be. Suddenly her musings were interrupted by the voice of Ralph, who was still standing behind her back. He walked up to her and put his hands on her shoulders. Amy involuntarily trembled at his touch.
- I bought the house even before we were married. - Ralph finally admitted. At the word wedding, Amy abruptly turned to him and looked into his eyes.
- Did you buy it? - Amy wondered aloud. She saw an implacable expression in Ralph's eyes. She knew that what he was saying now was important to him.
- Yes. - He finally admitted while wandering his eyes.
- Why didn't you say anything? - Asked Amy although she didn't know why she had squeezed out the question. Was it relevant now? Ralph hadn't mentioned it to her for a year, maybe he just thought he didn't need to, and yet she wanted to know the answer.
- I wanted to give you this house as a wedding gift. - He replied with a thoughtful expression. He walked past Amy and sighed deeply. Amy continued to look at him intently.
- I had hoped to spend our wedding night here, but in the end, it turned out differently. - He replied, trying to hide the emotions he still had at the thought of their wedding. Amy only now realized that maybe then, if she had reacted differently to what Ralph had wanted to say to her just before their wedding, maybe

their whole marriage might have looked different. Yet she didn't dare to ask him about it now either. Nor could she admit how unhappy she was knowing that Ralph was seeing other women. Thinking about all this made her eyes glaze over. She preferred to keep silent about the whole affair.
She took a deeper breath so that Ralph would not hear it. With one hand, she wiped away a tear that inevitably ran down her cheek and blinked so that she wouldn't collectively cry.
- It's nice that you finally decided to show it to me. - She admitted in slight reassurance. Ralph suddenly turned to her and looked at her with a surprised expression on his face.

CHAPTER 11

Moments later, the evening seemed to promise to be very pleasant. Once Amy and Ralph pushed the unpleasant thoughts away, they both relaxed. It seemed to Ralph that the cottage he had purchased had begun to appeal to her. She slowly walked around it, looking at and admiring the decor that was there. She began to feel more at ease especially when Ralph went into the small kitchen where he prepared dinner for them. Amy couldn't help but peek into the bedroom. Now that she was looking at the cottage she knew for sure that there was only one bedroom. She sensed that Ralph would want to lie down next to her at night because he certainly wouldn't want to sleep on the sofa in the living room. It might seem comfortable for resting during the day, but certainly not at night. She had no intention of sleeping on it either. She opened the bedroom door and stepped inside. She was instantly stunned by the experience. The bedroom was completely differently decorated from the interiors of their home in Chicago. The pastel walls only added to the charm. She wondered if Ralph had decorated the cottage himself or if he had simply purchased it with furniture. Although if he furnished the entire cottage, Amy would have to admit that she liked the decor very much. And she wouldn't want anything to change. Upon entering the bedroom, her attention was fixed on the large bed. It stood opposite the door, which was made of wood painted white. Then her gaze was caught by the dark gray bedding with bright bows on the pillows. Immediately her thoughts wandered to the moment when she and he would go to sleep in that bed. Amy felt she was losing control of her thoughts. She took a step back and shook

her head vigorously to shake off these dreams. She thought it would be better to
She left the bedroom and went to explore the other rooms. Closing the door behind her, however, she regretted not going to the window to see what the view was of. Just outside the bedroom door, she smelled a wafting aroma from the kitchen that worked her appetite more and more. She thought she hadn't even realized that Ralph could be such a good cook, yet she had been living with him for a year.
Finally, she started looking for the bathroom until she spotted a door of some sort right next to the clothes closet, which stood next to the exit door.
She walked up and pressed on the door handle. She went inside and turned on the light. She concluded that the kitchen seemed to be small for the bathroom was quite large.
She immediately noticed the bathtub, which could accommodate two people at once. She stood there motionless for a while and then suddenly lowered her gaze to the floors. She noticed that black roses were painted all over the light gray tiles along from the door to the bathtub, pointing the way to the tub.
She lifted her gaze higher and saw that the same roses were also painted on the tiles on the wall. But there the roses are arranged in different directions while creating an image of chaos.
One might have thought that the bathroom was decorated in rather gloomy colors it was, but the lamps that were fixed between the tiles on the bathtub added an intimate charm.
Still, Amy didn't know if this was Ralph's fantasy alone and inclusive, but how was she supposed to ask him about it. If they were a normal married couple she would have asked him this question, but so she had to deal with her doubts on her own. She decided that it would be safer for her to go back to the living

room and wait for Ralph there. After leaving the bathroom, she wanted to head to the kitchen and see
how Ralph was doing with preparing dinner
However, on the way, her attention was drawn to the fireplace, on which stood two glasses of wine. She walked over and picked up one glass and smelled the alcohol content. At first, she thought that perhaps the two glasses had stood there before she and Ralph came here. However, the wine smelled like it had just been opened.
- I chose dry. - Ralph's voice rang out in the living room. Amy set her glass on the mantelpiece and turned toward him, who was standing in the living room with two plates. From a distance, she saw that it must be pork in a marinade until she was tempted to taste this dish right away. Ralph took a few steps and placed both plates on the table, then walked over to Amy, standing next to her. She involuntarily drew into her nostrils his scent, which stimulated her senses more and more deeply. Ralph picked up the glass that Amy had set aside moments ago on the fireplace and handed it to her, then reached for another
- Here's to a happy trip. - He said and tapped his glass against Amy's glass, who stood beside him as if mesmerized. Amy thought to herself that this promised to be a really pleasant evening.

Only a few hours were missing before dawn, and their marriage could have undergone a complete metamorphosis. However, all the time some misfortune hung in the air over them. The wonderful evening that Ralph had planned could become an unforgettable night. At the time when Ralph was cleaning
In the kitchen after dinner, Amy decided to head to the living room. She sat comfortably on the sofa, snuggling her face into the upholstery of the sofa. Her legs dangled in the air above the

floor. She hoped that a moment of solitude would help her collect her thoughts. She tried to close her eyes after a hard day, but couldn't fall asleep.

She opened her eyelids as soon as she heard Ralph enter the living room and sit down next to her. He moved even closer to her and began gently massaging her calves, which made her feel even more distracted.

- Are you tired? - She heard Ralph's voice after a while. It seemed to her that his words conveyed concern.

- A little, but I don't want to fall asleep yet. - She replied after a while. Ralph watched her for a while. He sensed that it must have been a really hard day for Amy. He smiled under his breath as if an idea occurred to him.

- If so. - He began uncertainly. - Then why don't we watch a movie or listen to music? I have quite a collection of records here," he suggested, hoping for Amy's approval.

- Mhm. - She sighed. - Maybe let's listen to something. - Replied Amy after a brief moment of thought. Ralph suddenly clapped his hands. - Great. - He commented briefly.

Suddenly it occurred to Amy that perhaps she had made decisions without thinking. Listening to music seemed innocent but at the same time something dangerous. She and her in that tiny living room on the sofa, with only mood music in the background. It was obvious what this could lead them to. She had no intention of spending another night with Ralph, at least not until she knew what their marriage would be based on next. She wanted to talk to Ralph about it, but certainly not tonight. Right now she wasn't ready for such a conversation. Ralph tried to get up from the sofa when he suddenly felt Amy grab his wrist. He looked at her and wasn't sure what he saw in her eyes.

- Wait. - All he heard was her voice. Then he slowly sank on to

the sofa. Amy let go of his hand. Ralph felt that he should sit
even closer to Amy. He moved closer
and unexpectedly he brushed his fingers against her cheek,
something Amy was completely unsuspecting of. He leaned
over her lips and was already so close that he placed a kiss on
them. He knew she would have let him. She was ready to accept
anything Ralph would offer her now. But the moment was
unexpectedly interrupted by Ralph's phone signal.
It was hard to disregard the call, as the signal became more and
more insistent. Ralph moved away from her. Amy began to
listen to the conversation Ralph was having on the phone. She
sensed that something bad must have happened, his facial
expression said so. He disconnected the call and after a moment
turned to Amy, who had changed positions and was sitting
comfortably on the sofa. Ralph looked at her with a cloudy
expression in his eyes.
- There was a burglary in our house, we must return there as
soon as possible. - After which he left. This completely shocked
Amy. There was a break-in? But what were they looking for?
And then Amy realized that Ralph didn't say too much, maybe
he didn't know too much himself either, but he preferred to say
just enough so as not to upset her unnecessarily.
And now they are on their way to Chicago, and they could have
spent these moments very differently. Amy was already
beginning to wonder if she could experience a little happiness
by Ralph's side?
Apparently, this question must remain unanswered. She glanced
at her husband, who did not take his eyes off the steering wheel,
but sensed that he must also have been concerned about the
whole matter. She wondered more and more in what condition
they would find the house once they were in Chicago.

It was already two o'clock in the morning, it was still dark when they drove onto their property. Ralph got out of the car first, and Before Amy. She had the impression that her husband had completely forgotten that she was with him, as he quickly ran home. When Amy entered the house from the hall she noticed the two bodyguards that Ralph had hired some time ago, only when she was in the living room did she notice that her husband was also already there. The bodyguards, upon seeing Amy, retreated from the living room and checked the entire garden to see if they could find anyone there. It seemed that the thief had left Mr. and Mrs. Jones' property for good.

Amy approached Ralph, who captured her gaze, on which fear and horror were painted. In the living room, all the furniture was tumbled. There was shattered glass everywhere on the floor. Amy guessed that someone had broken the glass door from the terrace with all their might to force their way inside.

- Is the whole house in the same condition too? - She asked in a calm tone. Ralph walked up to her and grabbed her hand.

- Don't. - Responsible.

- Only the living room suffered.

- And did anything die? - She asked again looking closely at the broken glass on the floor. Ralph swallowed his saliva with difficulty.

- Fortunately, no, maybe the security guards appeared nearby and chased the thief away. - He admitted keeping a stony calm. With fear in her eyes, Amy looked at Ralph, who also noticed her anxiety. He squeezed her hand tighter so that she felt he was right beside her.

- Why did someone do this? - Amy wondered in her mind.

CHAPTER 12

The next few moments after returning home were hard to endure for Amy. She couldn't find her place. She kept wondering who might have tried to break into their house and destroy the living room she had always loved so much. She didn't want to typecast anyone baselessly, but recent events didn't give her peace of mind. For who could hate her and Ralph so much. It even crossed her mind that maybe the revenge was carried out by one of Ralph's former mistresses, whom he had once abandoned. Or maybe the burglar could have been the last woman who called the house some time ago and asked about Ralph. That he was having an affair with her was certain, but did the woman in question just agree to let Ralph dump her? On the phone she seemed determined to do everything, at least she gave that impression. She wanted to ask Ralph about it all eventually, but she couldn't imagine asking him any questions about his affair.

She was simply afraid of the pain she might experience and the heartbreak she would surely have after talking to her husband. In the end, she decided that she should calm her nerves, which were taking away her logical thinking. Until she was suddenly horrified by her discovery. Someone who had tried to break into their house might have done it on purpose. At all, the burglar didn't have to turn out to be the woman Ralph had abandoned. Maybe it was a case of a madman who wants to poison Amy's life or a psychopath who recently escaped from prison. People's jealousy is frightening. And at that moment she felt so sad. Someone was trying to make her feel unsafe in the house where she lived. She guessed that this was probably the

intention of the perpetrator. She knew she couldn't let anyone do
that. She decided that she would gather her courage
and agree to promote the book in advance. She left the kitchen,
where she didn't even know how much time she had spent.
She stood still and looked out the window with the light off. She
felt so safe, she was convinced that no one would notice her in
the dark. She went to the living room, where Ralph was still
cleaning. She stopped for a moment to watch her husband
sweep up the broken glass. As soon as she had time to dawn out
of this reverie, Ralph suddenly turned and looked at her.
He wondered if Amy was feeling a little better yet. She took a
step toward him, and Ralph's eyes watched her carefully.
Finally, she stood facing him. She appreciated that Ralph was
trying to remain calm and composed. She didn't know how she
should start this conversation. She only glanced at the floor,
which Ralph had already managed to clean up.
However, she immediately turned her gaze to her husband,
sending him a forced smile.
- I'm glad you took such care of everything. - She said what
came first to her mind.
- Don't worry, everything is fine now. - Responsible Ralph put
down the floor-sweeping brush, which he leaned against the
back of the sofa. He then looked at Amy with a more
affectionate gaze.
- Ralph. - Amy began uncertainly.
- I wanted to tell you that I want to, start promoting my new
book. - Amy finally choked it out. Ralph's gaze became fixed.
- Would you like me to organize a book promotion for you? -
Ask still in slight bewilderment.
- Yes, I have thought it all through. I think I shouldn't close
myself off from the whole world. I can't be afraid, especially not
now. Ralph sighed heavily.

- Don't you want to? - Amy asked in a half-whisper. Ralph suddenly shook his head.
- Of course, I want to. It's a good idea. I just didn't think you were ready for it, especially in the current situation.
- I'll be ready if you help me and be there for me. - Assured Amy.
- Of course, I will be there for you. You don't even have to ask for it.
- Replied Ralph sending Amy a warm smile. After his words, she breathed a sigh of relief. Ralph grabbed her hand, which he then kissed. Amy felt that she felt really safe with him.

A few days later, Ralph held a meeting with journalists. Amy was to say a few words about her book, which she is writing. The evening promised to be quite interesting although Amy felt an anxiety in her heart that she could not describe in any way. She had a feeling that it had to do with public speaking after all, she hadn't given interviews in a long time. The entire press conference was to be held at *Books And Events,* a bookstore in the heart of downtown Chicago. Amy left home a few hours before the meeting with Ralph, who immediately left her at the bookstore, while he drove to the publishing house for a while. Amy, meanwhile, was getting ready in her dressing room. She wanted to focus on her interview with the reporters, but her thoughts kept wandering somewhere. She sat comfortably in a chair in front of a dressing table with a mirror. Moments earlier, a stylist came to her, who took care of her hairstyle, makeup, and outfit. Amy was able to relax during this time, but she immediately began to wonder why Ralph wasn't here yet. After all, he had promised her that he would be present during the meeting. Amy couldn't imagine that he might be missing. But what if he didn't make it in time to arrive? Amy

would not have been able to cope without him. In an instant, she would cancel the entire meeting and quit writing the book. As the stylist was fixing the last strand of hair that had unexpectedly slipped out of her updo Amy raised her eyes and looked at the woman whose figure was reflected in the mirror.
- Has my husband arrived yet? - She asked after a moment of silence.
- I don't know anything, but don't worry I'm sure she'll be here soon. - The stylist assured her. Amy sighed heavily.
- If you want I can check if Mr. Ralph has already returned. - The stylist offered, seeing the concerned look in Amy's eyes, who at that moment breathed a sigh of relief.
- If the lady would be so kind, I would appreciate it. - She admitted with a slight satisfaction in her voice. - Of course. - The stylist replied and left the dressing room. Amy was left alone. She was still nervous. In no way could she calm her nerves. In order not to wallow in further contemplation she reached from the dressing table for the notes she had written yesterday for today's conference. She started going through her notes trying to remember as much information as possible when she suddenly felt a strange feeling that filled her with more and more fear with each passing moment. Not only had Ralph not yet arrived, but the stylist who was about to return was also gone. Amy felt clearly that today nothing was going well with the plan. For a moment that lasted almost an eternity, she sat as if on pins. Out of all this, she was
afraid to turn around and
look in the direction of the door, but sooner or later she would have to do so and see if anyone was behind her. It occurred to her that what an irony. Exactly over a year ago, she also sat in one bookstore and was all alone in it. Just then as today,

something suddenly fell out with Ralph and he had to go run an important errand. He left her alone. And suddenly it occurred to her. - Could history be about to repeat itself again? - She thought, but in her heart, she hoped not.

But the unfamiliar smell that had begun to waft through the air a moment ago suggested otherwise. She didn't turn around, but she was sure she wasn't alone in the dressing room. Fear began to paralyze her, out of it all she wasn't sure what she could do. Nonetheless, in one swift movement, she looked toward the door, which was slightly ajar. She didn't remember if the stylist had slammed the door behind her as she left the dressing room. For a very brief moment, something flashed before her eyes. Some kind of shadow, she felt the wind, which unexpectedly appeared in the dressing room. She was sure that the silhouette that flashed before her eyes was strangely familiar. It was as if she had seen her before. And then she heard an even stranger noise as if something had tumbled down the hallway. She wasn't hallucinating, after all, the sound seemed real. In one motion, she put down her notes on the dressing tables without taking her eyes off the door and got up slowly from her chair. She walked to the door, which she opened wide with one tug on the handle. She looked out into the hallway. She looked first to the right but saw nothing there. She turned her gaze and looked to the left side of the corridor, at the end of which she noticed some unknown shadow, which then disappeared from her sight. She was sure by then that someone was in her dressing room and wanted something from her. Just who? He was watching her, but unexpectedly something flashed through it. And then she noticed an overturned table, on which stood a glass vase with flowers. Now the same flowers were lying on the floor among the broken glass from the vase. And the glass again. She burst into tears and couldn't stop the tears streaming down her cheeks. Out of this anxiety, she wanted to start screaming out loud, but at the last moment, she restrained herself. She could hear conversations coming from far away. She wiped her damp cheeks from crying with her hands and turned around. She looked ahead. She spotted Ralph walking toward her, talking to her stylist. The two were engrossed in conversation, while Amy turned all pale with fear. Finally Ralph, together with the stylist, stood in front of Amy. He bestowed a smile on her but immediately clouded overseeing the terror in her eyes. He touched his hand to her shoulder.

- Amy, dear. - He called out suddenly.

- Is something wrong? - He asked, although he already knew the answer to that question. He knows1 his wife and knew that Amy never dramatizes. If her eyes are filled with fear then something bad must have happened.

- Say. - He urged her and unexpectedly bestowed his gaze on the stylist, who was still standing next to him and said nothing. She also did not understand the whole situation.

Amy, hearing her husband's voice, breathed a sigh of relief. She closed her eyelids for a moment and then immediately opened her eyes and looked at her husband with an expression of relief.

- It is good that you are already there. - She replied. Ralph squeezed her shoulder tighter. He clearly felt that there was something wrong. He wanted to embrace her and hug her tightly. It seemed to him that Amy wanted that too. And almost embrace her already. Amy was starting to hug

to him when suddenly Ralph felt her inch stiffen. The expression in her eyes became still.

- Amy, tell me what's going on? Is something wrong with you? - Cried Ralph releasing Amy from his embrace. He tried to catch his wife's gaze and noticed that her vision had frozen. Amy stared fixedly at the corridor, or rather the figure that lurked there. Finally, Ralph turned around, looked in the same direction as Amy, and saw the same thing. At the end of the corridor, he saw the figure of a man. He immediately recognized who the stranger was, it was Carter MacDonald, who again began to run away from them. Out of concern, Ralph embraced his wife and pulled her close to assure her that she was safe.

The stylist also stared in the same direction as Amy and Ralph but still understood little.

After a while, Carter MacDonald was not visible in the hallway. Amy could breathe a sigh of relief, but she knew that this was probably not the end of her troubles with this madman.

- Amy. Let's go home. - Ralph suggested, sensing that an even greater tragedy could occur in moments.

He pulled Amy behind him hugging her tightly. They walked down the corridor toward the exit. The stylist stayed where she stood, still stunned by the whole situation. She didn't understand what was going on. Ralph led his wife into the hall, passing on the way to the room where the invited guests and journalists were sitting. One man in a gray suit was hanging around at the door. He was the owner of the bookstore, with whom Ralph was well acquainted.

The bookstore owner immediately noticed Ralph walking along with Amy. He approached them. Ralph threw him a look without

expression. He hugged his wife tighter, who hid her face in his arms.

- Apologize to everyone and say that Amy and I had to cancel the whole meeting. - Said Ralph, who was not going to explain anything more. The bookstore owner was puzzled by this, to say the least. The two passed the bookstore owner and were already heading for the exit when a man suddenly called out to them. - But what do you mean? - He was surprised, but Ralph together with Amy did not react. They walked out of the bookstore. They were already outside.

They were walking slowly down the stairs when suddenly Ralph's gaze was caught by a crowd of people who had gathered in front of the bookstore.

Ambulance lights and police cars flashed everywhere. Ralph at first wondered if the throng of people were Amy's fans, but immediately thought it looked like a completely different situation. He and Amy walked closer together to see what had happened. And he immediately guessed that something bad had happened. A man was lying in the street who gave no signs of life.

All he heard around him were stories from people who claimed that the man was drunk and that's why he threw himself straight under the wheels of a passing car. He turned his gaze and glanced to the left. He noticed how two policemen were interrogating the driver of the car, who was in front of the lying man. Surely this was the perpetrator of the whole tragedy. Suddenly Ralph's attention was caught by the victim's face. He recognized who the accident victim was. He swallowed his saliva with difficulty and everything was now clear to him. It was Carter MacDonald. Amy's stalker. He ran straight under the wheels of an oncoming car just after Amy spotted him in the bookstore. And it was Amy. Ralph embraced his wife even more tightly, who did not seem to realize

the whole matter of the current situation. She was sort of in a trance,

Completely terrified that her stalker was again disturbing her peace of mind. Hugging his wife tighter, he stroked her hair. He didn't want to say anything to her for now. He thought it would be better that way. He would explain everything to her at home once Amy was feeling well. And then he heard some murmuring. Several journalists passed him and Amy. They took out a camera and started taking pictures of the late Carter MacDonald. Amy still seemed stunned. Ralph knew he had to get his wife home from here as soon as possible.

CHAPTER 13

The previous evening when Amy and Ralph returned home, Amy fell fast asleep. Ralph decided to keep vigil with her all night. The next day, at breakfast Amy still seemed silent and absent, and it remained that way until late in the afternoon. Ralph sensed that she would be better off confessing the truth about what had happened to Carter MacDonald as soon as possible. He wasn't sure how Amy might react to the news. He could see how thoughtful she was. She was sitting on the sofa wrapped in a blanket. Her face was pointed toward the terrace door. Ralph

He wondered if Amy was aware that Carter MacDonald was not a threat to her? He wasn't entirely sure because of the shock she had suffered yesterday. For a few moments more, leaning against the frame of the kitchen door, he watched his wife thoughtfully. Then he suddenly broke away and walked over to her. At first, he had the impression that Amy was asleep, but as soon as he stood in front of her he noticed that her eyes were open.

He sat down in a chair next to his wife, who suddenly tore her gaze away from the terrace and looked at Ralph.

- Amy. - Ralph dared to start uncertainly. Amy took a deep breath. She tried to be calm but sensed that Ralph would probably guess how shaky she was on the inside.

- I know you want to tell me something. - Amy spoke up, trying to start the conversation first. Ralph took a deeper breath. Amy corrected herself on the sofa.

- You don't have to say anything, I know what happened yesterday. - She admitted with a raised head. Ralph swallowed his saliva with difficulty. It was unbelievable. Amy knew everything, and he was still figuring out how to tell her.

- Do you know about everything? - Ask with concern in your voice.

- Yes, Carter MacDonald is dead. After he ran out of the bookstore he fell under the wheels of a car. Ralph lowered his gaze to the floor and combed his hair with his fingers. However, he immediately looked at his wife.

- Why didn't you say anything? - He asked.

- I had to think it all through. - What was that?

- So much has happened starting with our marriage. A year ago I went through hell. - Admitted Amy looking straight into the eyes of Ralph, who tried to read as much as possible from her gaze.

- This man tried to destroy me. He escaped from prison and still wanted to harm me. He was in a bookstore, from which he escaped as soon as I spotted him, and died shortly after. Understand, I felt to some extent guilty about this.

- You were not guilty. You didn't do anything.

- I know, but everyone will think of it that way, that he died because of me.

- What are you talking about? What everyone? - Ralph was even more surprised. And then Amy pulled out today's newspaper from under the blanket. Ralph decided not to buy today's paper. He was afraid of what he might read in it. He was convinced that the journalists would surely mention the tragedy that happened in front of the bookstore. Maybe someone would even recognize Amy's stalker as the victim of the accident. What he couldn't assume was that she would be the one to come out of the house to buy a newspaper. As Ralph tried to collect his thoughts, Amy handed him the newspaper. On the very first page, he noticed a photo of himself and Amy. What he didn't notice was how they took it. The headline of the article, however, hurt him more: the press conference with Amy Jones was canceled - the reason: the death of her stalker.

Ralph had to read the headline twice to be able to come to his senses. At the time Amy touched Ralph's hand with hers, he turned his gaze to her. She was so close to him then. He smelled her scent again. Amy vowed to herself that she would not break down, or rather, she would now be the one to support her husband. Completely different from a year ago.

- Make some tea so we can talk calmly. - She suggested in a calm tone that gently gave solace to Ralph's nerves. He nodded, put the newspaper down on the table in front of him, and went to the kitchen. Amy leaned with her back against the back of the sofa, as if she was really going to wait for the tea. She couldn't relish the moment of solitude for too long when she suddenly heard the doorbell ring.

She turned her head and looked to see Ralph pacing around the kitchen. She got up from the sofa and moved toward the door. As she passed

She shouted only to Ralph - I will open. But she did not notice that Ralph nodded, because she was already next to the door, which she then opened. She was startled to see Cora standing on the other side.

- Hi Amy. - Threw the woman suddenly.

- Hi. What are you doing here? - Wondered Amy, who covered herself even more with a blanket.

- Forgive me for bothering you. - Cora admitted.

- But I couldn't wait. I had to come and explain everything to you. - She spoke as if she couldn't stop the torrent of words. Amy didn't understand even more what her friend could mean. She seemed tired as if she had been up all night. Because maybe

she was, too. She had been pondering for too long, so now she didn't have the strength to keep up with her friend.
- But what to explain? What do you actually mean? - She asked completely indifferently. And then Cora took out today's newspaper from her purse.
- I read what happened. - Cora began uncertainly.
- Ah. you already know. - Amy breathed a sigh of relief.
- Yes, perhaps my fault. - She admitted with remorse in her voice Cora.
- How is it your fault? - She asked.
- Why don't you come inside and explain everything? - Suggested Amy, who was already ready to let her friend inside. - No, no, no. - Denied firmly Cora smiling lazily. - I don't want to disturb you and Ralph. I will explain everything and disappear. - She admitted but felt that Amy did not believe her. - Then say. - Demanded Amy in a firm tone. Cora took a deeper breath and looked at her friend, who was becoming increasingly
she was impatient. - A few days ago I met Ralph as he was leaving the restaurant. We talked for a while and.
- I.. - Amy urged. -Meet Lucas there and it was from him that I learned about your problems. - She finally confessed to Cora. Amy took a deeper breath.
- And what does all this have to do with the article? - Asked an increasingly nervous Amy.
- Then, in the restaurant, a journalist who was sitting next to our table must have heard our conversation. He probably watched you later. Sorry, I didn't mean for it to come out like that. Amy shook her head and a thought suddenly came to her mind. She looked with a more determined look at her friend.
-Was your meeting with Lucas a coincidence? - She finally asked Amy. Cora didn't know what to answer at first. However, continuing to hide the truth didn't matter.

- You're right, no. Me and Lucas have been meeting for some time. - Admitted Cora lowering her gaze to the ground.
- How come, and you didn't tell me anything. For God's sake, Cora after all we are friends. You always know what's going on in my life. - Started to say Amy with a slightly raised voice. - Forgive me, I didn't think everything would turn out this way somehow. - Assured Cora looking at her friend.
- What about your husband? Does he know about your affair? - Asked Amy, who seemed outraged by her actions.
- Mitchell is going to Australia. He wanted me to go with him, but I refused. It was to be a forever trip with
Chicago. - Cora responded by looking away. Amy suddenly realized what choice Cora had to make.
- In any case, this is the end of my marriage. - Confessed Cora after a while, glancing at Amy again.
- I have no regrets. Me and Lucas want to be together. - She added when she suddenly noticed Ralph approaching them. He put his hand on Amy's shoulder, who glanced at her husband.
- I'm going to go now. Take care, Amy. Bye, Ralph. - Added Cora, who suddenly turned and walked away. After a while, Cora's car could be heard driving away. Ralph closed the door after which his wife's gaze was directed at him. Amy swallowed her saliva. She suddenly felt that everyone had let her down, while she had always tried to be honest with them.
- Did you hear our conversation? - She asked without taking her eyes off Ralph.
- Only part of it. - Admitted Ralph, who guessed what Amy would want to ask him about in a moment.
-So. - Amy began nervously.
- Did you know that Cora and Lucas are having an affair with each other? - She asked while looking closely at her husband.

Ralph was silent for a moment and then spoke up. He had no intention of deceiving his wife.

- I didn't know, but I guessed that they were meeting.
- And you didn't say anything to me, why? - Amy was outraged.
- What for? - Ralph was surprised. - Cora should be the one to tell you, not me. - He admitted and started heading toward the living room.
- Tea is already waiting. - He added while Amy was still standing. She knew that in this Ralph was right. It was not him, but Cora who should tell her. But she didn't, could it be that she didn't trust her, after all, they were friends.

It's been two weeks since Cora dropped in for an unannounced visit and confessed that she was having an affair with her publisher. Since then, she hasn't spoken to her and hasn't even tried to contact her. Amy figured she wouldn't call her herself first either. She was feeling a little better by now, as the affair with her stalker had quieted down.
Journalists took up other topics. All that was left for her to do was to finish writing
books and arranging a continuing relationship with Ralph. She felt that her marriage had stalled and didn't know how she should remedy this. However, she hoped that today she and Ralph would be able to talk calmly about their future going forward. They were scheduled to have lunch together. Amy drove to the publishing house. She was a little ahead of schedule, but she didn't care.
She knew that Ralph might have a meeting at this hour, but in the end, she decided to wait for him at the office. Entering the publishing house, all the employees greeted her on the way very warmly. Apparently everyone remembered her well. Amy sent

them warm smiles. Entering the large room where all the editors worked, she noticed that at the

A desk by a large window is occupied by Jackson, whom she has not known for a long time. Next to him stands a blonde-haired woman with loose hair that flowed down her back. It was Cora. Amy at first wondered whether to approach them or not, but finally approached, this

more than Jackson noticed her. - Hello Amy. - A man called out suddenly. Amy, with a slightly disgruntled expression on her face that quickly disappeared, approached him. - Hello Jackson. - Amy replied while keeping her distance. At this point, Cora turned around and holds her friend's warm gaze.

- Hello Amy. It's great that you stopped by. - Cora spoke up.

- Hi. - Threw Amy, to whom this was the only thing that came to mind. She looked away then looked back at Cora and Jackson.

- What are you doing here? - Amy asked suddenly.

- Mhm... I help Lucas publish a little. - Cora admitted.

- Great news. - She replied blithely to Amy. Cora didn't know if Amy's answer should make her happy. Jackson listened to the chilly conversation between the two women.

- Forgive me, but I have to jump out for a while and get something done. - He threw suddenly sending a questioning look on Cora's face. He sensed that some kind of wall had been born between the women. He decided that it would be better for Cora and Amy to talk alone, backed off, and left.

- What's up with you. How is the work on the book going? - Cora asked. - Everything is going well. I'm slowly finishing it. - She replied.

- I came to Ralph's we have an appointment. We are going to lunch. - He is in the office. He is talking to Lucas. If you want to go to him. - Thanks. - Threw Amy after which she turned

around and started heading towards the study. - Amy. - Called out suddenly Cora. Amy stopped and turned toward her friend.
- Yes? - She asked.
- I just wanted to tell you that I know you resent me.
- Let's not talk about it now. - Amy suggested.
- Yes, but I should clarify that you may think I have something against Ralph, but that's not true.
- Why go back to that? - Amy asked. She didn't feel like talking to her friend about her marriage.
- She just knew before that Ralph has had numerous affairs, but now really change. I want you to be happy. I know you deserve it. - Good. That's good to hear," she said. - She chuckled to Amy and was already about to retreat when she heard Cora calling her again.
- Amy. - A woman's voice rang out.
- Yes? - She asked in a more assertive tone. Amy thought she was about to explode if Cora mentioned anything about her marriage again. She had had enough of that already.
- What are you doing on Saturday next week? - Cora asked.
- I don't have any special plans. - Answered Amy feeling visibly relieved. - Maybe you and Ralph could come over to our place. We're throwing a party at our new apartment. There will be some friends. - She wondered for a moment if Amy would accept the invitation.
- Sure, we will definitely come by. - Said Amy sending her friend a warm smile. - I'll text you the address.
- I'll be waiting. - She added in conclusion after which she turned on her heel and walked to the door of the study, where Lucas continued to talk with Ralph. Cora hoped that Saturday's party would help bury all resentments and they would continue their friendship with Amy.

CHAPTER 14

Amy walked up to the office door in a better mood. At first, she wasn't thrilled to have met the publishing Core. But now she felt they could make friends again, and that helped her put the past two weeks out of her mind.

Before she pressed the door handle, she thought she'd better knock so as not to disturb the conversation. However, she noticed that the door was slightly ajar. She wanted to go inside however something stopped her. She began to listen to the conversation, especially since the voices of both men were raised. The conversation she was listening to moved her quite a bit.

- Ralph, you know very well that we cannot keep delaying the promotion of your wife's book. - We'll hear back from Lucas first.

- Rest assured, we will be on time with everything. - Ralph assured.

- Sales need to jump up significantly. Those few scandalous articles in which your wife's name appeared helped a little, but you need to pull it further. - Suggested Lucas, who strolled back and forth across the office.

Ralph leaned against the desk and watched his partner closely.

- Let's wait until Amy just submits the text to the publisher and we can move on. - Admitted in a poised tone Ralph, who thought that everything was just a matter of time. Amy froze after those words. The conversation outside the door still continued, but she could not hear what the two men were talking about. Now that she had slowly begun to hope to live together beside her husband, she realized that Ralph did not love her. She heard it clearly from his mouth; he only cared about

selling the book he was writing. That brief moment was enough for Amy to understand that there was no point in their marriage. She moved away from the door with her heart beating hard. It felt like it wanted to jump out of her chest. She left the publishing house absorbed in her thoughts. She knew what she had to do, it would be better if she left first than when he decided to end this fiction. On her way out of the main hall No one even noticed her getting into the elevator. Descending to the first floor, she took her phone out of her purse and turned it off. She didn't want to hear the ringtone if Ralph spoke.
She decided to return home. She was right. Ralph called her several times. He was surprised and even worried that Amy did not speak to him. She was always so mindful of everything, and today she forgot that they had made an appointment. For an hour Ralph waited for her at the restaurant they planned to go to and kept calling her but the signal was off. Then he returned to the publishing house and only there did he learn that more than two hours ago Amy had been in the office asking about him. Only now Ralph was beginning to wonder what had happened.

Amy, meanwhile, had managed to pack her things. She had already ordered a cab, which was due to come for her any minute.
For the first time in her life, she regretted not buying an apartment with the money from the sale of her books. Now at least she would have somewhere to go. For now, she was going to return to the town where she grew up. Her grandmother's sister still lived there, so she hoped to stay with her for a few days and then find something for herself. She carried the last suitcase down from the floor to the lobby.
She figured there wasn't that much of the stuff she had collected over the past year, after all, she had only managed to pack in

two suitcases. She sat down on the sofa and started waiting for the cab. She knew she was doing the right thing. Unexpectedly, she heard the door open. She never imagined that Ralph would want to go home early. He immediately spotted the suitcases. He walked into the living room and aimed an implacable gaze at his wife, who was sitting on the sofa.
He took a deep breath and put both hands on his hips.
-Now explain to me what all this is supposed to mean? - He began in a firm tone. Amy only glanced at him and then got up from the sofa. She walked over to the suitcases that had been set up and tossed them carelessly on end. She wanted to end this matter quickly.
- There is nothing to explain. I am simply leaving. I'm leaving, I'll send you the divorce papers in a few days. I think it can be carried out somehow quickly. - She answered and tried to pull the suitcases behind her. What she didn't expect, however, was that Ralph grabbed her forearm at the last moment, aiming a cold stare at her. Amy tried to jerk out of his grasp but he held her quite tightly.
- Sorry, but there's probably a cab waiting for me by now. - She chuckled as Ralph's fingers tightened on her forearm.
- Let's get everything straight first. What is all this supposed to mean? - Ask heavily irritated. Amy watched his gaze for a moment. She felt Ralph suddenly loosen his grip.
- I want to end this farce. - Farce? - Ralph was surprised.
- Yes, there is no point in pretending any longer.
- What the hell are you talking about. - growled Ralph, who could not pretend to be calm.
- How about this. Don't pretend. I heard your conversation with Lucas. I know you only care about selling my book. You do everything to make it financially profitable for you. I have no intention of being stuck in such an arrangement any longer. -

She said in conclusion then jerked her hand harder.
Unexpectedly, Ralph let her go, and Amy at that time pulled out
one suitcase forgetting the other, and headed for the door. At this
time Ralph realized what Amy was really about. He scratched
his beard with one hand and heard Amy open the door.
- Wait. - He called suddenly after her.
- Please don't go away. - He added and turned in her direction.
He saw Amy about to cross the threshold of the door and leave
and never come back here again. This was his last moment to
stop her.
- Amy. I love you. - He said these words for the first time in his
life. Amy stopped, she could not cross the threshold of the door
without reacting to Ralph's confession.
- Stay with me, please, I can't imagine life without you. Talking
to Lucas has nothing to do with how I feel about you.
- He added hoping that Amy would believe him. These were the
words she had waited so long for. She was afraid she would
never hear them from Ralph's mouth in her life. She turned
around slowly and looked at her husband uncertainly. Suddenly
she forgot about his conversation with Lucas.
- How long have you loved me? - She asked. Now at the
moment, these words were the most important for her.
- I think from the moment I first saw you. And I certainly
understood it the day we got married. Amy sighed heavily and
closed her eyelids for a moment, but immediately opened her
eyes.
- And you. How do you feel about me?
- I'm in love with you, too, but I didn't want to tell you, because
I was afraid that with this love I would have to remain alone. -
She confessed with therefore in her voice. Her eyes became
glazed. She turned her head so Ralph wouldn't see her tears, but
he was well aware of them. Now he understood how much pain

Amy must have endured while he was dating and romancing different women. He walked up to her and put his arms around her waist hugging her tightly. Amy struggled to look into his eyes.

- I love you and from now on I will never let you down again.

- He added while placing a kiss on her lips, which Amy also reciprocated.

9 788839 659865 3